PRAISE TO THE MAN

LARRY BARKDULL

DESERET BOOK COMPANY

SALT LAKE CITY, UTAH

Library of Congress Cataloging-in-Publication Data
Barkdull, Larry.
    Praise to the man / by Larry Barkdull.
       p.   cm.
    ISBN 1-57345-320-X (pbk.)
    1. Phelps, William Wines, 1792–1872–Fiction.   2. Smith, Joseph, 1805–1844–Fiction.   3. Mormons–History–Fiction.   I. Title.
PS3552.A6166P72   1997
813'.54–dc21
                               97-39831
                                CIP

Printed in the United States of America

10 9 8 7 6 5 4 3 2   8006

To Dee Jay and JoAnn Bawden,
true friends of Joseph Smith, the Prophet

The author is a fool who thinks he can do it alone. Making books is a team effort. Thanks to Sheri Dew, Eileen Kump, Richard Peterson, Richard Erickson, Gary Swapp, Dee Jenks, Wally Wright, Keith Hunter, Celia Benson, Bronwyn Evans, and Margo Lunt–a publishing team extraordinaire.

CONTENTS

PREFACE

THIS FICTIONAL NARRATIVE, although it relies on historical facts, is not intended to retell history. For purposes of accuracy the author has made use of a variety of works cited in the endnotes, including *Missouri Persecutions* by B. H. Roberts and *Joseph Smith and the Restoration* by Ivan J. Barrett, and the serious student of LDS Church history will want to consult these and other historical treatments for factual information.

The primary purpose for writing this book has been to dramatize an inspiring though little-known relationship—that which existed between the Prophet Joseph Smith and his sometime antagonist and sometime loyal friend, William Wine Phelps. *Praise to the Man* recounts the rise, fall, repentance, and redemption of a great Mormon pioneer, and, in the author's opinion, no other story from Church history demonstrates better the far-reaching and saving power of the Atonement of Jesus Christ. It is also true that few other incidents in Church history provide a more

PREFACE

intimate glimpse into Joseph Smith's character. The
Prophet is shown in this instance to have been the
perfect embodiment of pure Christianity. In Phelps's
perfidy and Joseph's willingness to forgive is found
the Prodigal Son story of this dispensation.

Special thanks to Bruce Van Orden for his gener-
ous sharing of materials on William W. Phelps.

CHAPTER 1

MARCH 12, 1872.[1] OF THE hundreds of stories I have written as a journalist, this will likely be my biggest failure. I doubt that it will ever grace the printed page. Still, knowing the futility of my effort, I take pen in hand and attempt to reduce to writing the thoughts that have captivated my imagination these last weeks. I expect that when I have finished I will file my notes in a bank vault or some other cold depository. One thing is certain: my publisher will not understand why I will have nothing to show for my extensive travel time on this assignment and the expenses I have incurred visiting the deathbed of W. W. Phelps in the Great Salt Lake Valley.

Washington Irving Talesford[2] is my name. The Washington Irving part was laid upon me without my consent by my wishful father some fifty-eight years ago. He had loved Mr. Irving's writings and harbored a hope that his son, if so named, might rise to that author's stature. However, journalism, not literature, became my passion. The new state of Missouri

1

provided me an opportunity to chronicle the growing pains of a place and a people situated on the western border of the United States. I moved my young wife there, contrary to her desires, from comfortable Pennsylvania to live on the frontier. As for my writing career, I must have shown an ability early on. After publishing a few initial articles in obscure journals, the *Kansas City Examiner* offered me a meager position in 1832, and I have written exclusively for that paper ever since.

My journey to Salt Lake was uneventful, and only a few memories stand out. I attempted to pass the long hours spent riding in the stagecoach by engaging a newly married couple seated opposite me in light conversation. I learned that the young groom, Canterbury Deeber, I believe he called himself, hailed from the Oregon Territory. He was unfettered in his public demonstrations of affection for his new bride. He said he had purchased an acreage in the Northwest where he intended on settling with his wife to produce apples and children. Observing his gangly features, I decided that it would only be a matter of time before love, good food, and gravity would take their tolls. The pale skin pulled across his bony face revealed scant evidence of a beard. *One less thing to occupy his time*, I thought. He had a difficult time finding a place to store his oversized feet, which were caught in a knot of spindly legs. He looked warm for February, which intrigued me.

Mrs. Deeber—Belle—affected to hold an embroidered kerchief in her left hand. She was a blooming thing, maybe seventeen and healthily plump. She had bound her hair back into a tight bun, which I imagined would have had the bulk to cascade to her waist if liberated. Whenever we retreated from the stagecoach for a rest or a break, I noticed that Mrs. Deeber stood a palm's length short of her husband's bony shoulder. Her ample figure was confined in an uncomfortable-looking dress, built by an aunt, she said, expressly for her honeymoon trip. Its voluminous skirts were ill-suited for wear in the tight confines of the stagecoach. I could see, however, why the long groom had fallen in love with the lass. Her beauty would have attracted the attention of polished gentlemen in the most elegant cities, and she doted on her husband, allowing his amorous pecking without shame.

My seat companion was a fat man from Minnesota who sold blacksmith tools. He labored as he talked, struggling to take sufficient air into his massive chest. Although the temperature on the plains was cool, his coloring was constantly ruddy and his face was bathed in a constant flow of perspiration. A network of red capillaries lay on his cheeks and around his nose, appearing engorged and ready to burst. His trousers hugged his fleshy legs and were two sizes too small, I guessed perhaps sewn by an optimistic wife in one of the man's leaner seasons. To his disgust,

Mister Collier, as he called himself, as though
"Mister" were his given name, had made this trip
annually for the last eight years. The Mormons are
good for a few sales, he observed on a number of
occasions, but California is where the real money is. I
would nod as though I was interested, then go back
to watching the Deebers nibble on each other.

When I could stand my fellow travelers no longer,
I would retreat to a cold seat atop the coach beside
our driver, Herringbone Applegate. There, I would
ignore his attempts at conversation and survey
instead the broad prairies and diminishing frontier.

Herringbone had a foul tongue and cursed his
team of horses in an ongoing dialogue. He chewed
his tobacco with new teeth he said he had bought in
Denver last fall, where he was certain he had been
taken advantage of by a shifty dentist. He lamented
that he had saved up for the contraptions a full year
and complained that the blamed things made clack-
ing sounds when he talked and fell out without warning. He covered his balding head with an ancient,
sweat-stained hat with the brim turned up in front.
He apparently shaved at infrequent intervals, which, I
presumed, was also when he bathed.

As for me, I was a conglomerate of my fellow travelers. I am old, it is true. But I have more energy than
Mister Collier, who appeared to be twenty years my
junior, and less pep than Canterbury Deeber, who
was just a pup. Although not the size of Mister

4

Collier, I have managed to gain enough weight to require suspenders and am able to grab an admirable amount of my belly and mold it as a woman kneads dough. My hair has thinned over the years, as did my father's, and what is left has turned a pleasant gray. I am somewhat taller than average and have a deep voice, both of which are assets I have used to my advantage when interviewing difficult subjects or attempting to gain an edge on my competition.

I believe I might have had a wonderful trip except for my companions. Being a writer, the sights of the untamed prairies and mountains inspired a spate of descriptive prose such as I had seldom allowed myself to pen. My profession demands quick writes in response to inflexible deadlines—hardly art. But the sheer breadth of the virgin land, wild and open, untouched by man, captivated me and made me feel alive. I saw buffalo herds the size of a Missouri county, sweeping the plains, cutting a swath of broken ground, leaving the earth void of vegetation.

A burst of cold air pushing east drove me from my seat next to Herringbone, back inside the coach, to the company of the huffing Mister Collier and the amorous Canterbury and Belle. The weather confined me there for a week. Watching the Deebers, though, reminded me of a loving time some thirty-eight years past that brought me Ellen. I suppose that for a season we were as giddy as the newlyweds who cuddled across from me. One can live on love for a year, I've heard. Ellen and I tried, but bread became important. Poverty, coupled with weeks spent away from a young bride in an attempt to establish a career, worked devastation on our marriage, and I entered the ranks of the divorced. In spite of our problems, Ellen and I managed to produce a daughter, Kathryn, who lives near her mother, stepfather, and stepbrothers and sisters, in a plush section of Philadelphia. I've not seen my daughter since she was five. She would be middle-aged now, married, and a mother. I send her letters at Christmas, but I've never received a reply. If she hates me, I would not be surprised. I expect I would feel the same toward a parent who chose his career over his child. As I age, I find myself wishing I had been more wise.

The storm broke at last and yielded to clear, sunny skies as we drew nearer to Utah. I entertained myself with the hope that I might soon enjoy some Rocky Mountain sunshine.

Shortly after I began work at the *Examiner*, I was assigned to cover the frenzy over the "Mormon" issue. Reports of a strange sect with a new Bible captured the imagination and stimulated the fear of our readers. The Mormons had settled in Jackson County, primarily in the town of Independence.[3] They had arrived there by the mandate of their twenty-five-year-old prophet leader, Joseph Smith, who alleged that the land was the ancient site of the Garden of Eden and taught that a holy society called

Zion, or the New Jerusalem[4], would be built there. The area of Independence was one I had traveled, and, having seen it, I could not imagine anything so preposterous as Joseph Smith's proclamations about the place. Without question, the land was comely, covered with gentle hills, carpeted with ample grass and fed by abundant water. But, beyond its obvious fertility, Independence was only a rustic settlement, hardly worthy of the Almighty's attention to single it out as the home of humanity's first parents. At least that was my observation.

Joseph Smith had taught otherwise, and his followers had sacrificed all they possessed to migrate there as immigrants and pioneers, heaven-bent on building a modern-day utopia. None of this escaped local scrutiny and prejudice. As a reporter, I felt myself bound to remain neutral on such subjects, but I found myself siding with the original residents: the Mormons were strange. And a strange people are often a feared people.

Here I make note that the *Examiner* had been peppered with reports of outlandish behavior by the Mormons. A superstitious populous was ready to believe any exaggerated hearsay of happenings on the Missouri frontier. In most cases such accounts were investigated and discarded as so much gossip. Had Mormonism been just another upstart religion making fantastic claims, my newspaper would have shoved the story in a drawer and waited out the sect's demise, as usually happened. But Mormonism was blazing in Missouri, and reports swept through the state—of a people with horns on their heads, molesting the old citizens, and committing other atrocities. What was worse than the vicious imaginings was the fact that the Mormons had grown enough in number to affect the outcome of local elections. Then, too, they espoused such a different lifestyle from other churches that deep resentments seemed destined to follow them anywhere they might locate.

The Mormons were primarily Easterners, people whose customs and even dialect were different from the Missourians. From the beginning that did not bode well for them. In addition, Mormons were non-slave owners who opposed the practice, which excited strong feelings in a community that tolerated and protected slavery. Finally, vicious prattle coursed through local rumor arteries that the Mormons kept up a constant communication with the Indian tribes on the frontier and declared from their pulpits that the Indians are numbered among God's chosen people, destined by heaven to inherit with the Mormons the land of Missouri.[5]

The event that first took me to Independence, in 1833, centered on one William Wines Phelps—W. W. as he preferred to call himself (I never could; I liked to call him William)—and the destruction of his printing press. Mr. Phelps was nineteen years my senior—a newspaperman, as was I. At that point in time, he was seasoned in his profession, and I was just beginning mine. But our professional kinship made for an immediate rapport.

We may have been alike in vocation but not in appearance. In contrast to my early girth and receding hairline, both of which gave me the appearance of being older than my twenty-one years, William stood tall and angular, with a full fleece of dark, thick locks. His high cheekbones might have suggested an Indian progenitor, had it not been for his chalky white skin. I doubted that ladies' circles would have labeled him handsome. But, he was an imposing man, well-educated, direct, with an impressive command of the language. I could see that he would have been an asset to any organization fortunate enough to attract his loyalty.

I first met him in front of his destroyed home, where he was picking up scattered type and print galleys from the street. A rabble of citizens had formed a mob, attacked Phelps and his family, leveled his house, and trampled underfoot the freedom of religion and speech provided him by the U.S. Constitution.[6] That the Mormons were able to excite such passion in their neighbors increased my fascination with the group. William was courteous but haggard. He appeared worried about the safety of his children. As we spoke, we were often interrupted by messengers bringing him news of other displaced Mormons, an indication that Phelps was a leader among his people.[7]

From that initial meeting with W. W. Phelps to the present, I have followed the Mormon phenomenon with acute interest, and I have researched that people with perhaps more enthusiasm than any reporter on the *Examiner's* staff. I suppose that is why, when my editor learned of Mr. Phelps's failing health, I received the assignment to travel to Salt Lake City and attempt a last interview. I am sure the *Examiner* hoped for a deathbed, anti-Mormon declamation that might serve to refuel the local sentiment. That would have been understandable, since Mr. Phelps's defamatory writings had been published on the pages of our paper some years earlier.[8] In any case, with sparse notice, I found myself on a westbound coach to Utah, in company with the affectionate Deebers and fat Mister Collier, destined for the home of William Wines Phelps in Salt Lake City.

When William first saw me, he raised himself from his bed and greeted me as the old acquaintance I was. "Washington, you look as bad as I feel," he joked. His was a neat, quaint, adobe house that he had constructed when he and his family arrived in Salt Lake in 1849. It was located in a part of town called Old Fort.[9] He lay in a sunlit room, as genial and warm as the pleasant weather outside. His window was cracked to let in fresh air and the bustling sounds of a thriving city. Someone had embroidered "The Glory of God Is Intelligence" onto a framed linen that hung on the wall above the headboard of his bed. The room was well-kept. There was a grouping of apothecary pills and potions organized on a bedside table. A glass half-filled with water was nearby. The room was too small to be the master suite, and from the colorful walls and lacy white curtains, I divined that the apartment had belonged to a daughter and that William had been moved there where he could feel the sun and see the sights of the city through his window. A corner of the room was devoted to books shelved in a cherry wood case. That they carried no dust said the volumes were used or, at least, cared for.

"It's been a long time, Mr. Phelps," I replied. "Do you feel up for an interview?" A remnant of the man I had known occupied the relic that lay before me. His bony face was a sallow color, and a labored wheezing accompanied his breathing, which sounded painful. A thin sheet covered his withered body outlining the skeleton underneath. His once full head of hair was turned gray, the few strands that remained lying in an unkempt heap on a pasty skull. Suddenly, I felt guilty for having imposed upon the dying man, feeling that what I had to ask might figure in his imminent demise.

He responded to my question with unexpected strength. "Call me William, please, and yes, I have been looking forward to your visit." Without prejudice, he bounced between addressing me as either "Washington" or "Mr. Talesford." I answered to both.

He pointed to the two men who had guided me to his room. They were both dressed as if they were pall-bearers and looked as uncomfortable as I felt. "I hope you won't take offense. I've asked Avery Campbell,[10] from the *Deseret News,* and my son Waterman[11] to witness our interview."

I took no offense. I knew his concern. The national media, including my newspaper, had been known to skew the statements of prominent Mormons. Although William and I had developed a long relationship of trust, we both knew that I had no editorial control over the final printed page. I extended my hand to Waterman, William's oldest son. He was handsome. Tall and lean, he carried himself with dignity. I supposed him to be about my age. That he was a family man, I deduced from his references to his children and grandchildren. I admired his dark hair—a thick, dark mass of ringlets falling to his shoulders. He kept a dark, trimmed beard that hinted of silver and a little red. Waterman could have been his father when I first knew him, and watching the son attending to his father's comfort recalled for me my experiences with the Mormons in Independence, Missouri, in 1833.

Soon after meeting the Mormons, I had determined that none of the evil rumors I had heard about them was true. To their credit, they had transformed a harsh land settled by a rough lot into a charming community. Rows of pretty little farms and cabins dotted the landscape and filled the town. The Mormons, although an impoverished people, had brought with them an ethic of industry that had formed an economic base for the entire populace. As far as I could see, the whole community was prospering.

Mr. Campbell of the *Deseret News* eyed me. He shook my hand coolly but made an attempt at politeness. He stated that he had followed my career over the years and thought it was . . . *interesting*. His message was clear, and I was surprised that my writings were known in the Rocky Mountains. I accepted his comment as a compliment although I suspected it was otherwise intended.

Mr. Campbell, I discovered, was a seasoned reporter, who had learned his trade from writing stints at eastern newspapers before he joined the Mormons and migrated with his wife to Utah. He appeared to be in his early fifties—about ten years my junior—medium built, graying at the temples, and sporting spindled spectacles. He had the look of intellect over beauty, although I suspected he had been a striking man in younger years. I was intrigued by the shock of hair that lay as a lonely island on a sea of bright cranium. He had a habit of twirling it when conversations tensed. Aside from that solitary tuft, only a narrow band of hair wrapped around his head just above his ears. After we had exchanged pleasantries, we took assigned seats around the bed of a most remarkable man.

"I would like to make a statement," my subject began. William turned in his bed to face me. "I suppose your purpose in coming is to hear my denouncement of Joseph Smith and The Church of Jesus Christ of Latter-day Saints." I shifted uncomfortably in my seat. "I doubt that a Missouri newspaper would make the effort or expend the money for any other purpose, especially on a soul as poor as I. So, I will tell you in advance that you will leave disappointed. You need to decide if our interview should end now."

I looked at my counterparts sitting across from me. Waterman coughed and seemed to worry about something on the ceiling, and Mr. Campbell stared at me without blinking and wound his hair. "You are as astute as ever," I replied to William. "It is true that the *Examiner* hoped to ascertain your sentiments since—"

"Since I once wrote a condemning affidavit that was used in open court against Joseph and the Mormon people," he completed my sentence.[12]

"Yes," I answered, then added, "and because it is rumored that you had been excommunicated a second time."[13]

"A little problem with President Young and the fact that I took a polygamist wife without going through proper channels," he laughed. "I got my hands slapped and was rebaptized two days later."

I could see that William intended to be truthful and if anything of a sensitive nature existed in his past, he was willing to share all in the spirit of accuracy and in the defense of his beliefs. "All right," I conceded, "this is your interview. I will write it as you dictate. But you must allow me to ask some hard questions. Agreed?"

He nodded.

CHAPTER 2

I WAS BORN AND NAMED WILLIAM Wines Phelps on the 17th day of February, 1792, at Hanover, Morris County, New Jersey. My father, Enon Phelps, and my mother, Mehitabel Goldsmith, moved to Homer, New York, in 1800. I married Sally Waterman on April 28th 1815, and together we produced ten children. Early on, I developed a love for journalism and printing. I worked as editor of the *Western Courier*, I founded a publication called *Lake Light*, and I published the anti-Masonic *Ontario Phoenix*."

I knew something of William's background. His intellect and writing ability had launched his career. He had a passion for politics and had run unsuccessfully for lieutenant governor of New York state. While employed as a newspaper editor, William had settled with his wife, Sally, and their young family in Canandaigua, New York, just eleven miles from Manchester, the family home of Joseph Smith Jr. It was there that the Phelpses were residing when young Joseph received the golden plates in 1827.

Because of his journalistic background, William stayed abreast of the major events and local clamor surrounding the rise of Mormonism.[14]

William continued, "In 1823, the same year Joseph Smith had first gone to the hill to see the plates, the Lord prompted me in a dream to believe in the discovery of ancient gold plates, which would contain more plainness than the Bible. I rejoiced at this new knowledge—something that would point the right way to heaven. Then, in March 26, 1830, I read in the *Wayne Sentinel* from Palmyra, just twelve miles away, that The Book of Mormon had been printed by Egbert B. Grandin, and was now for sale. On the 9th of April, I bought a copy of the Book of Mormon and sat up that night with Sally reading it and comparing its teachings with those of the Bible.

"Over the next months, my feelings of joy grew concerning the Book of Mormon and the restoration of the gospel," he said. "By December 1830, I could stay away no longer. I sought out Joseph Smith on Christmas Eve day at the home of Peter Whitmer Sr. in nearby Fayette, located about eighteen miles east of Canandaigua. My faith increased as the grass after a refreshing shower, when I, for the first time, held a conversation with our beloved brother, Joseph, whom I was willing to acknowledge as a prophet of the Lord."[15]

William went on to relate that his attraction to Mormonism landed him in jail on trumped up charges of indebtedness. While in prison he wrote a public letter decrying those who had incarcerated him. William re-enacted for me the passion of his denunciation. "Is this religion? Is this liberty to jail someone who is investigating the truth? Is this humanity?" After a week he was set free without having to stand trial, but his experience in prison taught him where his true friends would be found—among the Mormons. Upon his release, he resigned as the editor of the *Ontario Phoenix* and moved to Kirtland, Ohio.[16]

Waterman Phelps looked alarmed when his father raised his voice. The son stood and reached for a bottle of medicine, but his father waved him off. Waterman returned to his chair, and Mr. Campbell craned to see what I was writing. I shifted away from him and into the sunlight.

William continued, counting for me the cost of leaving his printing business. "I spoke with Sally and the children about our move to Ohio to join the Latter-day Saints," he said. "Our break from our former life and security would be complete, with no looking back. We gathered what we could, and on the 9th of June, 1831, we left our home in Canandaigua and by evening we had boarded a boat on the Erie Canal, bound for Buffalo. We sailed by schooner to Fairport, Ohio, and from thence traveled overland to Kirtland to seek out the Prophet Joseph Smith. In truth, we had mixed feelings—sorrow for our present plight, but hope in Christ for a new beginning. We arrived on the 15th of June and sought out the twenty-five-year-old prophet of God. At that meeting, I announced I was willing to do the will of the Lord, and I petitioned Joseph to ask God his will concerning me."[17]

William motioned to his son to hand him the book of Doctrine and Covenants. "When my family arrived in Kirtland," he said, thumbing the pages of the book, "Joseph was preparing a select party to travel to Missouri to find the land of Zion by revelation."[18] William paused and lifted himself on his elbow so that he could look at me directly. "You have heard the term?"

"Zion?" I knew the word. "Yes."

"Do you know its meaning?"

"I know it is referred to extensively in scripture," I replied, "but I gather from your question that you have something to add."

William shifted to make himself more comfortable. "It is the heavenly society, the celestial kingdom where God and Christ dwell. All prophets and holy men from Adam to Noah, from Abraham to Moses, from Elijah to Jesus Christ, down to Joseph Smith, have longed for and dedicated themselves to preparing a people for such a society."

"You mean to build a holy city," I interrupted.

"Not exactly," he corrected me. "Zion, you see, always exists—it always has. It comes to a prepared

19

person or group of people who have espoused its doctrines. We cannot go to Zion on our own accord. That journey is made by direct intervention of God."[19]

William appeared to see that I was struggling to understand. I thought the whole idea was mystical, if not outrageous. William offered some descriptive language that helped. "Our covenant is twofold: first, to build up the kingdom of God on the earth—that is, the Church, which is preparatory—and second, to establish Zion—that is what we prepare for. In the days of Enoch, Zion was established by a people who had separated themselves from the world, ideologically, philosophically, spiritually, at the outset, then later physically and temporally. When they of Enoch's city had made and could keep the covenants of Zion, Zion came to them and absorbed them into that celestial society. That Zion existed upon the earth did not change the fact that it dwelled independently and separately from the world."

I saw William sink, and Waterman rushed to his side to steady him. The father rested against his son's arm and continued with these words: "When God calls a prophet and establishes a people, His aim is to exalt them and to establish Zion among them. Thus, from the beginning Joseph dedicated his life to teaching the saving principles of the gospel and to planting that vision of Zion in the hearts of the people."

Waterman helped his father sip from the glass of water then laid him back on his pillow. William winced at the movement. I could see that his effort to make his point had cost him in pain. He shifted until he found a restful position, then resumed his account. "My request to 'do the will of the Lord' was rewarded with these words." He handed the Doctrine and Covenants to me and bade me read Section 55.

I began, "Behold, thus saith the Lord unto you, my servant William, yea, even the Lord of the whole earth, thou art called and chosen." As I continued to read I learned that William was promised that after he was baptized he would receive a remission of his sins and then the Holy Spirit by the laying on of hands. He was told he would be ordained an elder by Joseph Smith so that he could preach repentance and baptism. I read further, "Verily I say unto you, for this cause you shall take your journey—"

"To Missouri," William interrupted to clarify. I nodded and resumed, "with my servants Joseph Smith, Jun., and Sidney Rigdon, that you may be planted in the land of your inheritance to do this work." William explained that his land of inheritance in Missouri was in the land of Zion and that the work referred to was William's assignment to assist Oliver Cowdery, the Second Elder of the Church, in doing the work of printing and selecting and writing books for schools in the Church.[20]

When I had finished reading, William asked, "Can you imagine sitting in company with Moses, Elijah, Jeremiah, or one of the other prophets and receiving personal instructions from the Lord of the whole earth?" I was struck by the reverence in his voice. "Joseph Smith was a prophet of God just as holy men in ancient times. The English language has not the power, and I have not the skill to express, the joy I felt when the God of heaven spoke to me through his chosen servant."

These special callings, I was told, meant more sacrifice for William's family. They were to stay behind in Kirtland and be cared for by the Saints while William made his long journey to Missouri.[21]

I closed the book, and as I handed it to him I looked into his lined face. Thus was converted, I realized, one of the most influential Latter-day Saints in the early days of the Church: William W. Phelps.

Mr. Campbell took the Doctrine and Covenants from William and fingered the pages. "The idea of modern-day revelation is a hard one for you, isn't it, sir?" the *Deseret News* reporter said, without looking at me. His statement was a challenge, not a question. "You see it as the vain imaginings of a fanatical people."

I surmised by Mr. Campbell's tone that the role he was to play in the interview was that of antagonist. Such rivalry was not new to me. I was used to being challenged. Journalists, I had learned, take up sides of a debate with as much passion as do lawyers. Mr. Campbell's assignment seemed to be to watch for signs of my turning against William Phelps and the

Mormon people. I didn't mind the wariness, but I was curious as to why Mr. Campbell just plain didn't like me. I glanced at Waterman and William, who seemed interested in how I would answer their companion's question. I sensed myself very alone in the room, as if my response would determine whether the interview would proceed or end suddenly.

I impressed myself with my diplomacy in answering Mr. Campbell. "The concept of contemporary communications with the heavens is both intriguing and foreign to me. That the Mormon people have so thoroughly embraced it as fact and have been willing to sacrifice to such extremes speaks well to their belief. As for me, I am as yet one of the admiring uncommitted."

Mr. Campbell raised his eyebrows at my response and seemed satisfied. "Very political," he observed. "I wonder if you have thought of running for office?"

I amazed myself again. "You're too kind," I lied, "but then I would be loathed by all the people, not just the half that now clamor for my resignation." It was a joke. William laughed. Waterman smiled. Mr. Campbell retook his chair.

I resumed questioning William Phelps. "Why were you and your family willing to pay such a price?" I asked.

"We knew the Book of Mormon was true," stated William, relaxed. "It is the pearl of great price that, once found, a man will give up all he has or is to possess. By that book I learned the right way to God; by that book I found the new covenant; by that book I learned when the Lord would gather scattered Israel; by that book I saw that the Lord had set his hand the second time to gather his people and place them in their own land; by that book I learned that the poor Indians of America were remnants of Israel; by that book I learned that the New Jerusalem, even Zion, was to be built upon this continent; by that book I found a key to the holy prophets; and by that book the mysteries of God began to unfold before me, and I was made glad."[22]

CHAPTER 3

I STOOD AND SHOOK THE BLOOD back into my sleeping leg. "So you went to Missouri," I said, trying to move the conversation along.

"That's right."

"I remember Independence as being nice, but not much to look at," I said.

"Maybe you had no vision," Mr. Campbell countered. The Phelpses nodded at the reporter's assessment.

"You may have a point," I conceded. Still, the idea of Independence as the location of the Garden of Eden and the future home of the New Jerusalem was one I could not fathom.

William's expression said that he understood my unbelief.

"It's all true." He emphasized each word. "Everything Joseph revealed about that area is true. I was there. I know that land, every part. When the original elders went along with Brother Joseph to seek the land of Zion for the gathering of the Saints in the last days, I was in the little band. I knelt with Joseph and the others when that goodly place was consecrated. When the first house was raised, I helped carry the first log. I preached the first Sabbath discourse to the Saints in Jackson County.[23] I offered the opening prayer when the temple site was dedicated. I traveled with the Prophet. I heard him lay before us the latter-day glory of Zion where the city of New Jerusalem would be built, the home forever of the pure in heart, the abode of God and of his Christ. I saw the vision—all we who came to that land saw it—and we were determined to give all that we were or had to establish Zion in our day."

"Bold words," I commented. I had tired of weighing each syllable. "Some have said Missouri was the vision of a fallen prophet, a charlatan." Waterman leaned forward in his chair, and Mr. Campbell reached for his clump of hair.

"Not true!" William stopped me. His hard swallow should have reminded me to be more careful in speaking with the sick man. "Joseph was a prophet of God. What he taught us was right. We, those of us who lived in Jackson County, fell short in living what he taught."[24]

"Tell me, then," I challenged, softly. Mr. Campbell's eyes flashed a warning. "You were there, as you say—an eyewitness. Perhaps few knew Joseph Smith as you did. But why should anyone believe he was any more than the numerous other teachers of religion who profess a dispensation from God and lead their followers as sheep into dumb subjection?"

"Your style is as keen as ever, Washington," William chuckled, whose levity appeared to surprise his companions. "You challenge my every word trying to raise my passion. You look for the unspoken message. As one newspaperman to another, I congratulate you. Still, you might have a little pity on a man so close to leaving this world. I hope when you write your summation you will print what I say and not give too much license to editorializing."

I relaxed. William Phelps was no stranger to debate and positioning. I smiled my acceptance of his terms. I began to understand that he had granted the interview for his own purpose, not mine. That he had something to say had become obvious. But, he had yet to tell me something new. His history and the accounts of the persecuted Saints might have been obtained in libraries. He held his true objective close, though, obliging me to wait upon him and allow his story to unfold. When he looked satisfied, he stared past me, out the window, and continued his narrative.

"After my initial visit to Missouri, I left Independence for Ohio, August 9, 1831.[25] A previous revelation given through the Prophet Joseph had instructed me and my family to settle in Jackson County and assume the responsibility of printing for the Church.[26] At a Church conference held in Kirtland, September 12th, I was instructed to stop in Cincinnati, Ohio, on my return trip to Missouri and to there purchase a press and type. These I would use in the printing of the Church's monthly paper, which was to be called *The Evening and Morning Star*."[27]

"I've read some of the editions," I interrupted him. "Very professional. Is it not true that you were the editor of that publication and that it became the official voice of the Church?"[28]

"Yes to both questions," replied William. "And thank you."

Mr. Campbell smiled his approval.

I nodded. "Some say you became Joseph's pen as Sydney Rigdon became his voice," I added. "You, more than any other, wrote and interpreted the events of the rise of the Church. Would that not be an accurate statement?"

William squirmed. He brushed my adulation aside as best he could. "It is true, I suppose, that I joined the Church at a time when my particular skills as a printer and writer could be used by the Lord. My burden lay in describing with words the events that unfolded before us, events that prior to our living them had been seen only in vision by former holy men of God. However, my contribution pales in comparison to the Prophet's." William skillfully moved me away from personal congratulations to crediting Joseph Smith. "That I knew Joseph as intimately as any man could know another, that he loved me as a brother, that he had implicit faith in me as a man of God, having received that confidence by a vision of heaven,[29] was payment enough for me. I witnessed his countenance change when the Spirit of the Lord spoke through him. I sat with him in council as he explained the Book of Commandments that I and others were to prepare and publish for the Church.[30] Yes, I knew him, and I knew that everything he said was true."

"And you saw the Angel Moroni?" I queried.[31]

William paused and eyed me. Avery Campbell rose to his feet. "You are seeking a way to discredit this man as a visionary. You have no interest in spiritual matters."

Waterman added his view. "We know full well how my father's answer would be received by your readers."

I ruffled in my defense, annoyed that each of my questions was being dissected for motive. I had opened my mouth for a rebuttal when William spoke.

"Gentlemen, gentlemen. We are professionals here." Then he addressed me. "I offer my apology, Washington. I'm afraid that with notoriety comes the risk of misquotation. My associates are well-meaning but, perhaps, a little overprotective. I hope you can appreciate that a certain paranoia goes along with any interview that can impact the Church. Your representing a Missouri newspaper only serves to heighten that anxiety. Still," William continued, "I accepted your invitation for an interview because I have known you over the years and believe you to be fair." He motioned his two witnesses to be at ease.

"For the sake of our long relationship," he conceded, "I will answer you this: my spiritual conviction came as it does to every sincere seeker of the truth, by the gift and power of the Holy Ghost. Once in place, other manifestations of the truth follow those who sanctify themselves before God. I will state for your interview that my testimony is that Joseph Smith was a prophet of God and that he had all the experiences that he claimed. Furthermore, I will state that others were chosen to the holy apostleship who bore independent testimony of the reality of Christ, the calling of his prophet in the person of Joseph Smith Jr., and the restoration of the fullness of the gospel in our day. Beyond that, I would feel ill at ease revealing any sacred experience I may have had. Does my answer satisfy you?"

"Yes, sir." As a hardened journalist, I found myself embarrassed at my adolescent attempt to lead my subject. I apologized and turned to a new page in my notebook. "When you and I first met, you were hurrying to gather your family, along with the rest of the Church in Missouri, to escape into Clay County. Would you tell me the events that led up to that tragic time?"

"I will, sir," he agreed, "but first let me say that no

people came to a land with more purpose and rejoicing than did we who first came to the land of Zion. We missed being near to the Prophet, since he remained at Kirtland, which was then the headquarters of the Church. Those of us who had settled in Independence began the work of building permanent homes. We had arrived too late that first season to raise crops, but we cut hay for our cattle and prepared the ground for cultivation. Still, for all our industry, we were unable to provide shelter for the influx of immigrants. Through that long, cold winter we submitted to all kinds of inconveniences, such as several families living in an open, unfinished log room without windows and nothing but frozen ground for a floor. We mostly ate beef and a little cornmeal bread. But we felt a spirit of peace and love and promise.

"As soon as the Saints in other areas of the country learned that the Lord had revealed the location of the city of Zion, preparations to purchase inheritances absorbed the minds of the faithful. Money arrived from all quarters, sent to the Church agent to purchase lands. As the Bishop in Zion, Edward Partridge shouldered the responsibility of dividing the inheritances among the Saints."[32]

"It was there that the Church tried a form of communal living,"[33] I recalled. The idea was not new in the United States. Other religions, immigrants, and groups had attempted variants of the concept. Some had read of Christ's apostles organizing such a system in ancient times and endeavored to duplicate it. All tries by those various groups had failed, as far as I knew. I had always been intrigued by that part of Mormon history—the building of an utopian society—and the fact that William had been such an integral participant in the effort.

He began his explanation. "Joseph Smith had received instructions by revelation that there were to be no poor among us and that we were to consecrate of our property and resources to sustain those less fortunate."[34]

"Human nature would eventually push toward inequality," I observed.

"Yes," he agreed, "but Joseph mapped out the Lord's plan, which lessened that tendency." William then expounded on the system he and others had learned from the Prophet. "Stewardship rather than common ownership was the driving principle of Zion. Joseph taught us that the earth is the Lord's and everything on it. We consecrated our properties to the Bishop of the Church without reservation. In return, we received an inheritance, or a stewardship, from the Bishop. Stewardships were made by deed, and we could improve them as we pleased. By covenant, all had equal claim to the assets of Zion, but we were independent in the management of our personal stewardships. Our surpluses were to be given to the Bishop for the Lord's storehouse, not for our own aggrandizement. Times of periodic accounting and donating of surpluses to the Bishop were provided to ensure basic equality.[35]

"In a revelation from the Lord, Joseph recorded: 'It is not given that one man should possess that which is above another, wherefore the world lieth in sin.'[36] The Bishop's Storehouse was meant to be the control center of Zion, the place where the Bishop would take account of stewardships, manage surpluses, and distribute resources to those in need. In this way the poor were to be cared for and stewardships could be improved by drawing on the common resources of the storehouse."[37]

"An ambitious economic plan," I observed. "And you were willing to give your all to such a speculative venture?"

"I was a leader of the Church in Missouri. As you noted earlier, I published *The Evening and Morning Star* and wrote much of the editorial content. I wrote of Zion and, in a sense, I was Joseph's voice in Missouri[38]—his *written* voice, I should say. Yes, I gave gladly all I had to the establishment of Zion. I championed its cause and promoted Joseph's vision in word and deed."

From the corner of my eye I could see Mr. Campbell beginning to fidget. "My question was not a challenge," I said to William, "but I am astonished that you were able to dedicate yourself to such a difficult concept."

33

"Sacrifice is never convenient," William said, "but it always brings forth the blessings of heaven."

"But does the spirit of sacrifice make the principle less difficult to live?" I didn't let him answer. "I can see why the poor would flock to such a program. But what of the rich? Human nature being what it is, didn't a certain envy exist: the once-rich feeling that they were carrying the weight of the society; the once-poor still measuring themselves against those who had consecrated more? It seems every decision by the bishop would be subject to the closest kind of scrutiny as to whether everyone was truly living equally. And then even if money and property were removed as social divisors, what about influence? Was there not a risk that some would seek rank and attempt to move up the ladder of Church status? I can only suppose, sir, that even among the most well-intentioned of the human family, your idea of a Zion-like society would be difficult to live."

"Indeed," William mused. "You make your point and I cannot disagree. The Prophet directed Bishop Partridge to guard against freeloaders who might take advantage of the consecrations of others. Those wanting to come to Zion were instructed to pay their debts, husband their properties and savings carefully, and secure pure varieties of seeds and improved breeds of livestock to bring with them. Joseph said that if immigrants supposed that they could come to Zion without ought to eat, or to drink, or to wear, or anything to purchase these necessaries with, it was a vain thought.[39]

"We had our problems, it is true. Joseph warned us at every juncture. And our difficulties were made more acute by those we called brothers and sisters who left and betrayed us."

"You're saying the Mormons' troubles came from those who left the Church?"

"Those dissenters, yes, and also the envious clergy who called themselves the servants of Christ. They who have once basked in the light do not merely abandon the truth. They attack."

William asked for a glass of water, and Waterman rose to help him. When he had settled back on his pillow, I waited for Waterman's signal that I could resume. William spoke first. "Apostates," he muttered. "Simonds Rider, Ezra Booth, Eli Johnson, Edward Johnson, John Johnson Jr., apostates all.[40] And there were others. They joined us, supped with us, called us brothers in the cause of Christ. But when they left, they didn't just go back to their old ways. Their whole purpose in life became to incite bitter feelings, drive us from our homes, and exterminate us from the face of the earth."

For all our talking, we had yet to speak of William's defection from the Church. I had been sent to Salt Lake City with instructions from my editor to get the full story of that time in Mr. Phelps's life. His reference to apostates gave me an opportunity to broach the subject. "You speak as though you had first-hand knowledge." My voice was even.

Waterman looked away, concerning himself with a knot in a floorboard. Mr. Campbell coughed a warning in my direction and sought the tuft of hair on his forehead. William regarded me with steely eyes. "I'll give you and your readers your pound of flesh, but in my own good time. I know what you want, but I won't allow you to turn my words. You cannot understand what happened to me without knowing about those beginning years."

His rebuke worked, and I tried to defuse the tension. "Will you continue then?"

A palpable discomfort had settled in the room. I had tipped my hand too soon. I thumbed through my notes without looking at him and waited until he was ready. When he finally murmured, "Very well," my counterparts melted back into their chairs. Mr. Campbell tugged at his collar, found his handkerchief, and wiped his brow.

William began slowly, deliberately, as if he were tiring of the interview and had become frustrated by my company. "For a while we were as happy as any people who had lived upon the earth. We tried our best to live the principles of Zion, all the while assimilating a burgeoning population of Church members who had come to Missouri from across the United States and Canada. In the November edition of *The Evening and Morning Star*, we reported that eight hundred and thirty souls constituted the population of the Saints in Zion.

"Persecutions were constant. Some houses were stoned and their windows broken; many of the Saints suffered abusive language; and some of our crops and property were burned. Still, we tried as best we could to live in peace with our neighbors and deal even-handedly with them. The Lord blessed us with food and raiment, and there was plenty in Zion. The years 1831 through 1833 were eventful. We felt the doctrines of the Restoration distill on us as the dews from heaven. Our hope was constant that we were establishing the land of the New Jerusalem where Christ would come to usher in his millennial reign."[41]

William's voice picked up strength. "Then, a feeling of insubordination began in Jackson County with some of the priesthood leaders. Seven men, myself included, had been appointed to direct the affairs of the Church in Zion. Of our several responsibilities, one was to appoint other elders to preside over the respective branches. But a number of brethren outside the Church leadership ignored our authority and began setting in order the branches. This caused confusion among the Saints. In addition, some immigrants who came to Jackson County sought to obtain inheritances by other means than according to the laws that governed stewardships in Zion. Feelings of jealousy and a spirit of light-mindedness sprouted. A general neglect of keeping the commandments of

God kindled the displeasure of the Almighty. All this came to the attention of Joseph, in Kirtland.[42] You asked about human tendency toward greed. We were warned. Joseph addressed a letter to me dated January 11, 1833. As a leader, I was to communicate the Prophet's severe rebuke to the Saints in Missouri."

William pointed to a journal on the bookcase. Waterman retrieved it, and William opened the volume to a marked place. "Mr. Campbell, would you read this?"

The *Deseret News* reporter adjusted his spectacles and read aloud a letter above the signature of Joseph Smith Jr. Here I quote only part:

> Brother Wm. W. Phelps:
>
> . . . the Lord will have a place from which his word will go forth in these last days in purity, for if Zion will not purify herself . . . he will seek another people. . . . They who will not hear his voice must expect to feel his wrath. Let me say unto you, seek to purify yourselves, and also the inhabitants of Zion, lest the Lord's anger be kindled to fierceness. Repent, repent is the voice of God to Zion . . . hear the warning voice of God lest Zion fall. . . All we can say by way of conclusion is if the fountain of tears is not dried up, we will still weep for Zion. This from your

brother who trembles for Zion, and for the wrath of heaven which awaits her if she repent not.

Joseph Smith, Jun.[43]

Mr. Campbell closed the journal, and William continued his account. "A people as blessed as we had been were under solemn obligation not to treat lightly the knowledge and commandments of God."

When I asked if the people accepted President Smith's reproof, William said, "A solemn assembly was called, and a sincere spirit of repentance was manifested. He had told us that 'as strange as it may appear, yet it is true, mankind will persist in self-justification until all their iniquity is exposed.' We leaders drafted a general epistle, had it read to the Saints in Missouri, and sent a copy of it to the Church authorities in Kirtland. At a subsequent conference held in Zion, we expressed our desire to keep the commandments of God, and thus we began to repent, and the angels rejoiced over us. Still, there were many things in which we fell short and displeased God. We were soon to feel his chastisement."[44]

"So came the intense persecutions of the summer of 1833," I noted.

"Yes, sir," he responded. "So they came."

CHAPTER 4

I T WILL HAVE TO WAIT UNTIL tomorrow." That is how William answered my question concerning the Saints' expulsion from Jackson County. It was now mid-afternoon, and William needed rest. Waterman remained to tend his father while Mr. Campbell escorted me from the room. I thought maybe an effort at goodwill would help bridge the chasm between the *Deseret News* reporter and myself.

"I have appreciated your comments, Mr. Campbell," I heard myself say, "and if I have said anything to offend you—" He cut me short by asking if tomorrow at nine o'clock would suit me as a starting time. His voice was cool. I agreed to the time and asked him to point me toward the famed temple site. He made a quick gesture toward downtown Salt Lake and walked back into the house.

The temple block was not difficult to find. The entire community seemed to be focused on the construction area. At first, I thought that the domed tabernacle was the temple, but I soon discovered my mistake. The tabernacle had been completed, but the temple was still under construction.[45] I admired the building's perfect symmetry, which appeared to float above the high stone wall surrounding the square block.

The temple architect, Truman O. Angell, dropped his work to escort me on a tour of the site. I doubted that he submitted to every unscheduled interview, but the press can command privileges, I had found. When he was called aside, I was left in the company of Thomas Quinney, a Mormon convert from Kentucky. He said he had been employed driving a team from the quarry in Little Cottonwood Canyon until he had been asked to work on the Utah Central Railroad. He had helped on the construction of a railroad branch line east from Sandy that would reach the quarry next year, he hoped. Recently, he had moved his family from the community of Wasatch, near the quarry, into the avenue area of Salt Lake City.[46] He told me that his new assignment to work at the temple site in downtown Salt Lake City was the highlight of his nineteen years of labor on the temple.

"Joined the Church in 1831," he said, while he pointed out the benefits of a granite foundation. He related that he had moved from Kentucky to Missouri in 1832 and received as a stewardship a comfortable acreage on the eastern outskirts of Independence.

"Then you would know William Phelps," I interjected. "I am interviewing him for a newspaper article." The man I spoke with stood short, but lank as a scarecrow. His chin stubble would never grow into a beard, I surmised. His feet were too small for his body and made him appear as if he was continually trying to balance on them. His leathery face said he had labored outdoors most of his life.

"W. W.?" he responded. "Sure, I know him. I'm a singer, ya know." I didn't know, but had no reason to disbelieve him. "Sung ever' hymn W. W. writ," he bragged. "Guess I've sung 'Adam-ondi-Ahman'[47] in ever' ward in the Valley."

I acted impressed, feeling that by stroking Mr. Quinney's ego I might get some insight into my primary subject. "I understand Mr. Phelps served as a Church leader in Missouri."

"Yup."

"Could you elaborate?"

"Y'mean was he a good one? Sure. The best. He could expound on the society of Zion better'n any man, 'ceptin' the Prophet, I 'spose. He was part o' Zion's Camp, ya know." I didn't know that either, but I knew the term. Zion's Camp had been organized by Joseph Smith in Ohio to travel to Missouri for the purpose of redeeming Zion and reclaiming the properties lost by the Saints.[48] Mr. Quinney and I walked along the top of the temple foundation and gazed into the sixteen-foot hole.[49]

"Mighty deep," I observed.

"Lotta diggin'," he responded, "lotta rocks, lousy

ground. Break yer plow sure as Brother Porter totes a gun." There was a character I would have loved to interview on this trip—Porter Rockwell. I had always wondered if half what was reported about him was true.

I retrieved a plug of chewing tobacco from my vest pocket and gnawed off a bite. Mr. Quinney eyed me. "Don't suppose you want a chaw?" I said, offering him a black ration. He shook his head and answered that he used to chew, but it had rotted his teeth before he knew better, and Joseph had taught against the habit, anyway. I had suddenly embarrassed myself. In my enthusiasm to be relaxed, I had disregarded local custom. To his credit, Mr. Quinney didn't correct me, but I found myself in the awkward position of being unable to discard the wad in my mouth. I dared not spit tobacco juice in the sacred temple area, and I couldn't bring myself to swallow it. When Mr. Quinney was pointing to where three towers would be placed at the eastern wall of the temple, I found my handkerchief and rid myself of the gob.

From the top of the foundation, about eight feet above ground level, I could look over the wall and scan the city. For late winter, this seemed an unusually pleasant day. I had heard how fickle the weather could be in Utah and wondered if those who farmed fruit orchards might not regret this warm streak that had urged buds to prematurely erupt on tender branches.

Salt Lake's men wore hats and rough breeches. Many grew beards of varying lengths and styles. Such a quantity of facial hair would feel hot, I guessed. I wondered how wives could become accustomed to kissing husbands through the thickets. Evidently they had managed, for Salt Lake teemed with neatly clad children, as happy as I had ever seen. I thought the women of the city looked old, suggesting a hard life taming a wilderness and caring for families. Occasionally, I would spy a woman in a lighter-colored dress that gave the appearance of comfort and style. But, more often, I saw dark, thick material draped over weather-worn bodies, the apparel buttoned to the chin and trailing in the dirt. Bonnets and other headgear covered tightly knotted hair, which might have been beautiful if freed. It all smacked of modesty but not very much of fashion.

As I surveyed the city, I found myself berating the terrible waste of land Brigham Young had allocated to the streets of Salt Lake. For a people whom I had known to decry excesses with zeal, I was amused by the exorbitant width of the roads. What could he have been thinking? I almost laughed at this evidence of poor planning. Still, I was impressed that the city had been laid out precisely north, south, east, and west, with the temple block as the center. A visitor could find his way with little difficulty through the city just by knowing the points of a compass.

"The plat of the city warn't unique to Brigham

Young," Mr. Quinney said. "He followed the plans for cities Joseph Smith drew up."[50]

His tidbit of trivia caused me to survey the city once more until I came full-circle to Temple Square. I admired the temple's massive foundation hole and commented that the nineteen years it had taken to arrive at this point suggested a difficult project.

"Been challenges and delays," Mr. Quinney explained. "I helped cover the whole thing up in '58." He told me that U. S. military forces had entered the territory and that threat had motivated the Saints to cover the foundation with dirt and plow it over to disguise it as a field. When it was unearthed four years later, in 1862, inferior masonry was discovered. After some deliberation, President Young ordered the foundation dismantled and replaced with granite rock.[51]

"Did you do any construction in Missouri?" I asked.

"Some. Mostly farmed. Got burnt out in '33." Mr. Quinney appeared sad when he remembered. "Loved that little farm," he said. "Loved Missouri. Ya ever seen the Missouri River?" I nodded. "Purty, ain't it? Buried one o' my children there on its banks." I let him look away without pressing for details. After some silence he asked me if I had ever lost any family. I thought of a young wife who had given up on having a husband who would love her more than his career. I thought of a five-year-old girl placed on a buggy bound for Pennsylvania, crying that she would never see her Daddy again. I didn't rush to hold her one last time.

"Yes," I replied. That's all I said.

"I brought my fam'ly to Missouri to build up Zion," he remembered. "Martha 'n me 'n our two little boys and our baby daughter. We loved the Saints, but we had to endure some abuse from the 'riginal settlers—black-hearted ba—er . . . sorry. Some habits are hard t' break." I waved it off.

"We heard 'bout some o' th' brethren bein' beat, down by th' Big Blue River.⁵² 'Spected it were true. At meetin's we were reminded o' the persecutions suffered by the disciples of Christ in ancient days. Never figured we'd have to pay th' same price for the truth's sake. I recollect at Church conference, in April '33, we marveled at how the Church'd grown and how much'd been 'complished in just three years. We'd become thous'nds; the place of Zion'd been revealed; Brother Phelps had 'stablished a press and a Church newspaper. Guess our numbers 'n 'complishments scared th' Missourians—leastwise made 'em envious. Ol' Prejudice reared his ugly head 'n we were made to pay."⁵³

"Tell me about Will—W. W. Phelps," I requested.

"When the mobs came to drive us outta Jackson County, W. W. and five other men offered themselfs as a ransom for us,"⁵⁴ Mr. Quinney replied. "Guess he's 'bout as good a man as God's ever made. Joseph loved him like a brother, ya know. Trusted him with all o' us in far 'way Missouri. And W. W., he loved Joseph. No one could talk 'gainst the Prophet 'thout W. W. gettin' on his feet in his defense. 'Spose the most powerful testimony I ever heard of Joseph Smith was that'n of Brother Phelps. Me 'n Martha took in Sister Phelps 'n the littleuns," he added, puffing out a bit.[55] "Betcha didn't know that, neither." I hadn't. "Joseph needed W. W. in Kirtland, so he hadta leave his fam'ly in Missouri fer awhile. Took his boy Waterman with 'im.[56] We took th' rest in. Had an empty place in our hearts, anyway. Helped to be servin'. 'Sides, Brother Phelps'd done so much for us."

Mr. Quinney paused as though he were searching for another piece of trivia he could impress me with. "Betcha didn't know W. W. 'n Waterman lived in Joseph's and Emma's home in Kirtland th' two years they was away." I acted impressed. "Yup," Mr. Quinney strutted. "W. W. was a reg'lar part o' th' Smith's fam'ly."[57]

"But later, didn't he turn against all of you?" I pressed. "You must have felt betrayed."

Mr. Quinney's expression said he had forgotten he had been talking to a reporter. When he spoke again, he did so in a more guarded tone. "Yes, it was hard. I loved that man. All th' Saints did. But what we suffered 'cause o' W. W. was nothing compared to how much we prayed for him. We all loved him, ya' see." Mr. Quinney didn't elaborate, and I moved to another subject.

47

"What about your child who died?" I asked.

Mr. Quinney glanced away, then took a big breath. "She weren't but two. Started a fever that day, November 5th, if mem'ry serves. We were forced outta our house at gunpoint in the dead o' night. Martha pleaded with the mobbers to let us stay 'cause o' the baby. But I'd heard stories of the mob rapin' the women n' killin' the children, so I grabbed the baby n' wrapped her 's tight 's I could in a big blanket. Martha got th' boys, and we were herded like cattle into the muddy streets of Independence. We'd seen a pretty bad storm that day—the November cold'd made it worse. We ran to the banks o' the Missouri 'long with t'other Saints. I tried to make a shelter, but it didn't work much. By the 7th th' storm hadn't let up and th' banks o' the Missouri was filled with Mormons—thous'nds of us—runnin' from the mob, tryin' to 'scape into Clay County, 'cross the river. We were freezing. We daresn't go back to town fer fear that th' mob'd kill us. We just sat in the mud for three days, watchin' our town 'n homes go up in flames. Baby Sarah got worse. She burned with the fever n' coughed 'til the poor little thing couldn't breathe no more. The brethren blessed her, but she died that night."[58]

I gazed at my guide with growing admiration. "This is uncomfortable," I said. "We can change the subject."

Mr. Quinney put his hand on my shoulder and

looked at me. "It's all right. I think you should know. But you'll have ta fergive me, Mr. Talesford," I heard him say. "I ain't no educated man. Learned what I have from some books and an ol' aunt who didn't want no fool fer a nephew. I never learnt how ta say things purty, like they otta be said. I just want you to know I ain't got th' words to tell you how my ol' heart broke when I buried my baby on the muddy banks of the Missouri River. That black night in th' drivin' rain I 'spected my life was over. I loved that little girl so." I waited for him to compose himself. "But God gave me 'n Martha a miracle to show us he was near."

"A miracle? How so?"

"The only way 'cross the river was by ferry, 'n th' cost o' ferrying a family 'n wagons 'n goods was a dollar and a half. Some o' th' families had th' fee 'n some o' us didn't. I didn't. We was obliged to remain camped on th' Jackson County side of the Missouri River, constantly fearin' that th' mob'd kill us. Me 'n two other brethren decided to try'n catch some fish 'n see if the ferryman would 'cept 'em instead o' cash. Well, we set our lines one evening. The following day, when we pulled 'em in, we'd caught three small fishes and a large catfish. Can you 'magine our surprise when we opened the mouth of that catfish and found three silver dollars? That was just th' amount we needed to ferry our families to Clay County."[59]

I tried not to react, but I felt a rush of emotion. It must have caused my face to flush, for when Mr.

Quinney looked at me he turned away, seemingly embarrassed for me.

We parted after that. He directed me to a comfortable boardinghouse near Temple Square where I was given a nice dinner, even though they didn't serve coffee, and I slept well until morning.

CHAPTER 5

"BEAUTIFUL MORNING," WATERMAN Phelps observed when I mounted the steps of his father's house. "Smells new, as though spring's coming." He had discarded his formal clothing of yesterday and donned a more casual outfit. He took my coat and hat and bade me loosen my tie. I thanked him, adding that I would like to meet the person who had invented the necktie so I could give him a piece of my mind. We shared a comfortable laugh.

"How's your father feeling today?" I asked as we moved through the house. "Is he up to continuing our interview?"

Waterman smiled. "He was cussing all of us this morning. I guess he's doing all right. He's bound and determined not to go willingly. It'll take a whole legion of angels to get him out of here." I was beginning to like this man. In my research for the interview, I had read some of Waterman's compositions in Church magazines. He had followed in his father's footsteps to some degree and had developed a gift for writing.[60] His father cleared his throat, focusing my attention.

"Morning, William," I said, bowing slightly.

"Morning. Avery's been delayed. He'll be along soon. Something about a deadline at the newspaper."

I was relieved. Waterman moved my chair to the window where the morning sun could spill its warm rays on me. I thanked him and William began.

"I've been thinking I should tell you about the mob driving us out of Independence." I nodded and opened my notebook to a clean page.

"In April of 1833, some three hundred of our non-Mormon neighbors met at Independence to demand our immediate removal or, that failing, formulate a plan of destruction."[61]

I stopped him. "Where was Joseph Smith?"

"He was in Kirtland, but in contact with us." I jotted a note and William continued. "Reverend Finis Ewing, the head of the Cumerland Presbyterian Church, issued a statement saying that the Mormons were the common enemies of mankind and ought to be destroyed. Then, a Reverend Benton Pixley spent his time going from house to house spreading slanderous falsehoods in an effort to incite the people to violence. Early in July, a document known as the 'Secret Constitution' circulated through the county, enumerating alleged grievances the mob had suffered at the hands of the Mormons and binding all who signed it to assist in driving the Saints from the county. The signers pledged their lives and sacred honors! We were accused of being the dregs of society—lazy, poor, and vicious. Our enemies also spread rumors that we had incited slaves to rebel against their masters with bloodshed. The document stated that we must leave the county, and if we refused, we would be forced out."[62]

"You had the power of the press at your disposal, though," I said. "Surely you employed the written word to counter the accusations."

"Of course," replied William. "I tried to quell the passion in *The Evening and Morning Star*, but to no avail.[63] Another anti-Mormon meeting was held on the 20th of July. Four to five hundred people gathered at the Jackson County courthouse that time. Their intent was to devise a means to get rid of the Mormons. The charges against us were repeated, and this was the decision: that in the future, no Mormon would be permitted to move into Jackson County and that those of us who were then living there would have to set a date by which we would move away. In addition, I, personally, was required to cease publishing *The Evening and Morning Star* and to close the printing office altogether. I was also ordered, as a Church leader, to use my influence to see that these terms were carried out to the letter. As a concession, we were promised we would be unmolested if we complied. A threat of mobocracy and war was held over us if we resisted.

"The mob's committee called upon me, Edward Partridge, and the other leaders to make their demands known to the Church. Mr. Talesford, the task of moving and resettling over twelve hundred people, along with their livestock and belongings, plus the selling of properties and businesses for a fair value, would have been no small endeavor. We asked for three months to give our answer; we were denied. We then asked for ten days; we were given fifteen minutes. The demand was totally unreasonable. We were confronted with an impossible situation, so the meeting broke up, and the mob's delegation returned to the courthouse and reported that we would not give them a direct answer. At that point, the mob resolved to raze my printing office and destroy the type and press."[64]

I interjected a question. "I believe I first met you the day after your press was destroyed, July 21, 1833.[65] Is that your recollection?"

"Yes. If memory serves, you arrived in Independence on the 21st. John Whitmer directed you to my house."

"What was left of it, you mean."

"You are right, of course. Yelling like demons, the mob attacked my family, threw the type and the galleys of the Book of Commandments into the street, and destroyed our home. Sally escaped with one of our sick children in her arms. We were frantic. For a time neither of us knew the whereabouts of the other.

Two of our little boys were trapped in the rubble of our home, but by the providence of God, were uninjured."[66] I looked to Waterman, who answered my glance by saying that he was not one of the trapped children but had escaped with his mother.

William resumed his account. "Then the mob demolished the Gilbert & Whitney Store. They caught Bishop Edward Partridge and Charles Allen and dragged them into the public square. There they were stripped of their clothing, daubed with tar mixed with lime, and covered with feathers. The two men bore this cruelty with dignity and meekness, so much so that the crowd eventually grew still and allowed them to retire."[67]

I offered an observation. "While standing with you in the street, overlooking the ruins of your home, I remember seeing the lieutenant governor of the state walking among the debris."

"Lilburn W. Boggs," William affirmed. He didn't seem to enjoy saying the name. "Do you recall what he said to us and the other Saints who stood there surveying the destruction?" William answered his own question. "*You know what our Jackson County boys can do, and you must leave the country!*" William paused before asking, "Don't you find it curious that Lilburn Boggs was one of Missouri's largest landowners, especially in that part of the state?"[68]

William's recital brought to my remembrance the scenes I had witnessed that first awful trip I had

made to Independence. On the 23rd of July, a mob of
five hundred reassembled and burst into Independence, bearing a red flag and armed with rifles, pis-
tols, whips, and clubs. They rode in every direction
looking for William and the other Mormon leaders,
making the day hideous with their wicked oaths. I
heard the inhuman cry over and over: "We will rid
Jackson County of the Mormons! Peaceably if we can,
forcibly if we must. If they will not go without, we will
whip and kill the men; we will destroy their children,
and ravish their women!"[69] I recalled thinking that
few threats could be worse than utilizing brute force
against the helpless innocent. Murder, at least, left the
victim at peace in death. The foul threat of ravish-
ment, I was to learn later, would be fulfilled.

I remembered Thomas Quinney's recollection that
William and five other Mormon leaders had stood
against the mob and had offered themselves as a ransom for the people, willing to be beaten or even killed
to satisfy the tormentors and end the cruelties. Their
offer was refused, and they were told that every man,
woman, and child would be molested until they consented to leave the county. Leaving or dying were the
only choices. William and the other leaders had no
alternative short of innocent blood being spilt. Thus
they were forced into an agreement that half the
Mormons would leave by January 1834, and the
remainder by April of that same year. The mob
promised no further harm if the terms were carried

out. "Like bargaining with the devil," William observed. "The mob kept no agreement we made with them."[70]

"Was Church leadership in Kirtland notified?" I asked.

"Oliver Cowdery was dispatched to Ohio to recount the travesties perpetrated against us and to confer with Joseph and other leaders.[71] As Oliver hurried to Kirtland, some of the Saints attempted to settle in Van Buren County, but the residents drew up a document pledging to drive them out as well. They were obliged to return to Jackson County.[72] The guarantee of no further violence was short-lived. Daily the Saints were insulted, homes were broken into, and the people were threatened. Orson Hyde and I met with Governor Dunklin and presented him with a petition setting forth the Saints' sufferings and denying the allegations of the mob. We asked for the state's protection. We pled for redress for the damages to our property, for abuse, for defamation of character. We begged to be restored to the lands we had purchased with our own money and had beautified by our own industry."

"Governor Dunklin was a great speaker and made many promises, but, in the end, proved himself to be a coward. He referred us to the same judges who led the mob. They were the ones who had secretly sought the assistance of the lieutenant governor of the state, Lilburn W. Boggs. To say we were more than disheartened by Governor Dunklin's response would not understate our feelings."[73]

At his father's request, Waterman showed me a journal filled with documents describing the hostilities that followed. When the mob learned that the Mormons were preparing to seek civil redress, they made a proclamation that any Church member attempting to use the courts would pay with his life.[74] A contingent of fifty hostile men met on the 26th of October and voted to drive the Mormons from Jackson County.[75] On the 31st, the mob attacked a branch of the Church located on the stream called the Big Blue. They whipped several of the brethren nearly to death, drove helpless women and children into the wilderness in the middle of the night, then tore the roofs off and demolished ten to twelve houses. That fact corresponded with the account of Mr. Quinney. The following night, the settlement of Saints at Independence was invaded, along with the Colesville Branch in Kaw Township. On November 2nd, the mob returned to the Big Blue and again began the work of destruction.[76]

"Where was Joseph Smith during all this trouble?" I asked, closing the journal.

"You mean was he cowering in Ohio, leaving us to be driven and butchered?" William countered. Avery Campbell entered the room at that moment and stopped short of offering his greeting. I glanced at the reporter but kept my attention focused on William Phelps.

"You agreed to answer my questions," I reminded the old man. "One could infer that Joseph was conveniently absent while his people were being massacred in Missouri."

William was incensed. "I will answer you, sir. I fear by not doing so you will write your speculations as facts." Mr. Campbell had not sat, but stood, holding his hat in his hand and listening.

"You assume too much, William," I defended myself. "Because I ask you hard questions does not mean I am your adversary. You know the minds of my readers. If I do not ask, they will. But, without being presumptuous, which other journalist in Missouri has treated you as fairly as I? Did I not write an accurate report of the events surrounding the Saints' expulsion from Independence and even denounce the mobocracy? Did I not later publish your own words of denunciation of Joseph Smith and his followers? More than any other journalist, I have allowed you the latitude to vent your feelings publicly. You, yourself, have gone from being one of Joseph Smith's most loyal proponents to being one of his bitterest enemies. Now you represent yourself as a devoted disciple and refuse to utter a syllable against the man. Tell me, sir," my voice raised in passion, "which William Wines Phelps do you wish me to quote?"

Waterman stood to deflect my passion. "Have you no decency, sir? This man lies at death's door, and you dare to verbally castigate him?"

William raised his hand to stay his son's agitation, then spoke quietly. "Words well said and deserved, I fear." He looked at me. "Give me a few minutes, won't you?"

I nodded and stepped from the room.

CHAPTER 6

"WE ALL COULD USE A RESPITE," I said as I left.

"I'll go with you, if you don't mind," Mr. Campbell offered. I was surprised, but I retrieved my derby and walking stick and we stepped together off the porch into the streets of Salt Lake City. A night breeze had cleared the haze from the valley, and for the first time I had a clear view of the magnificent Wasatch Mountains. Some said these monoliths of the Rockies were the most beautiful in the majestic chain. I could not disagree. The morning air was crisp, turning our speech into visible puffs of air. But a bright sun promised to warm the valley by midday to the point that we might discard our coats. As I surveyed the snow-clad peaks, I imagined them to be a fortress, tall and elegant.

"Beautiful, aren't they?" Mr. Campbell observed. "I've been here since 1849 and never grown tired of looking at them. I've climbed most."

"Yes, they are remarkable," I agreed, still amazed that I was having a pleasant conversation with Mr.

Campbell. "At least I'll take this pleasant memory with me back to Missouri—an image of the Rocky Mountains." I paused. "The rest of the trip has been a disaster."

"How so?"

I considered that by answering, I was making Mr. Campbell my confidant. I decided to risk it. "There's nothing new here. Oh, I've learned a few new facts—anecdotes mostly—but nothing worth the long trip west. I'm not a novice when it comes to the Mormons, Mr. Campbell. I've followed their story since the early days in Independence. Mr. Phelps seems set on giving me information I could have just as well read in history books or journals."

"You'll be in trouble with your editor?" he asked. I nodded. "Editors," he muttered in disgust. I nodded again. Mr. Campbell and I walked along the wide streets of the city. He related that when the Mormon pioneers arrived here in 1847, this valley and the barren land to the west formed a desert that had been infrequently visited by wandering trappers and hunters. Little was known then of the great potential of the intermountain country. The few travelers who had passed through this land prior to 1847 had hurried on to the Pacific Coast. No one thought of occupying such a dry and apparently unproductive region. Jim Bridger, the scout, was so sure that the Salt Lake Valley would not produce a crop that he declared he would give one thousand dollars if he knew an ear of corn would ripen here.[77] His view was shared by others who were acquainted with the region.

After a moment, Mr. Campbell changed the subject. "You have assumed Brother Phelps still harbors bitter feelings against Joseph and the Church," he said. "You came expecting to obtain a sensational deathbed story—'With Dying Breath, Prophet's Friend Declares Mormon Founder a Fraud.'" He moved his hand in front of him as if his finger pointed to each word of an invisible newspaper headline. We chuckled together. I told him I guessed my trip had been a reckless attempt by an overzealous editor to get a story.

"Editors," we said together.

Outside the pressure of the interview, Mr. Campbell was proving himself a pleasant fellow. Strolling together, in relaxed conversation, we abandoned our roles as interviewer and nemesis. I found myself liking this man and even supposing we could be friends in different circumstances.

"You might enjoy this," said Mr. Campbell. We sat on a bench in front of a little shop, and he handed me part of a composition he was preparing for July publication. It was an excerpt from a journal entry by Wilford Woodruff:

> July 24, 1847: This is an important day
> in the history of my life and the history of

the Church of Jesus Christ of Latter-day
Saints. On this important day . . . we came
in full view of the great valley or basin [of
the] Salt Lake and the land of promise
held in reserve by the hand of God for a
resting place for the Saints upon which a
portion of the Zion of God will be built.
We gazed with wonder and admiration
upon the vast, rich, fertile valley which lay
for about twenty-five miles in length and
sixteen miles in width, clothed with the
heaviest garb of green vegetation in the
midst of which lay a large lake of salt water
. . . in which could be seen large islands
and mountains towering towards the
clouds; also a glorious valley abounding
with the best fresh water springs, riverlets,
creeks, brooks and rivers of various sizes
all of which gave animation to the sporting trout and other fish, while the waters
were wending their way into the great Salt
Lake. Our hearts were surely made glad
after a hard journey—from Winter
Quarters—of 1200 miles through flats of
Platte river, and steeps of the Black Hills
and the Rocky Mountains, and burning
sands of the eternal sage region, and wil-
low swales and rocky canons and stumps
and stones—to gaze upon a valley of such

vast extent entirely surrounded with a perfect chain of everlasting hills and mountains, covered with eternal snows, with
their innumerable peaks as pyramids towering towards heaven, presenting at one
view the grandest and most sublime
scenery that could be obtained on the
globe. Thoughts of pleasing meditation
ran in rapid succession through our
minds while we contemplated that not
many years hence and that the House of
God would stand upon the top of the
mountains, while the valleys would be
converted into orchards, vineyards, gar-
dens and fields by the inhabitants of Zion,
the standard be unfurled for the nations to
gather thereto.[78]

"That quote will be part of an article I'm writing
for Pioneers' Day," noted Mr. Campbell. I responded
that I liked it and asked for a copy. He said that since
he had the original, I might keep it.

We sat quietly, and I found myself laboring to ask
him a question. "You haven't trusted me during this
interview, have you?" I finally asked.

He took his time, then answered with a question.
"Have you ever heard of the miracle of the seagulls
and the crickets?"

I had read the famous story. In the spring of 1848,

the pioneers in the valley put in crops, which from the beginning promised a rich harvest. But in early summer a plague of crickets descended from the mountains and destroyed a great portion of the crops. Every effort was made to drive them off, whole families turning out to fight the pestilence until everyone was exhausted. According to the reports, the entire yield would have been destroyed had not the Almighty in his kindness sent vast numbers of gulls to devour the crickets. The miracle saved the lives of the colonists, whose hope of escaping starvation rested on the harvest of 1848.[79]

"Yes," I replied. "I know the story."

"Do you like seagulls?"

I answered that I thought they were graceful birds but sort of loud and obnoxious-sounding. I said I'd always viewed them as scavengers. I realized then that I might have tread on sacred ground. The seagull was a revered bird in Utah. Mr. Campbell appeared to sense my anxiety and said he felt the same way about the pesky fowls.

He elaborated. "I've always wondered that God used the bothersome gull to save the Saints. They are kind of like journalists who write on both sides of the fence, sometimes they're a blessing and sometimes a curse."

I sat surprised.

Mr. Campbell folded his hands between his legs and studied the gravel walkway at his feet. Then he uttered a soft, but cutting statement: "I know you better than you think, Mr. Talesford—or should I say, 'Henry Baum'?"[80]

I was astonished. First, I froze. Then I felt my face flush. Not knowing how to respond, I stood and paced. I tried to pretend I didn't follow his drift or recognize the name. All the while, he sat motionless, letting me rave. Finally, I realized my attempts at deflection were useless.

"You know?" I asked. "How?"

"Known for years," said Mr. Campbell, still studying the ground. "I told you I had followed your writings. Even under an alias, some peculiarities of style show through."

Stunned, I stood staring at him. Of all my readers, only this obscure *Deseret News* reporter had found me out.

"Sit back down, Mr. Talesford," he urged, patting a place on the bench.

I sat, studying a scuff mark on my shoe. After a time, I glanced at him. "You're pretty good," I commented. "What do we do now?"

"Nothing," he replied. "I've said nothing to William or his son. Brother Phelps remembers you as a friend. That's all right with me. But you asked me why I was suspicious of you. I'd like to tell you a story."

He began. "Henry Baum was Lilburn Boggs's devoted proponent in the press. Mostly, he wrote for the *Western Monitor* out of Fayette, Missouri.[81] At every opportunity, on every issue, Henry Baum sided with the lieutenant governor of Missouri. Baum began taking up the cause against the Mormons early in 1833. Do you remember this statement?" He drew a paper from his pocket and read a quote: "The Mormons are the common enemies of mankind and ought to be destroyed."[82]

I knew the words well. Under the pen name of Henry Baum, I had quoted the Reverend Finis Ewing, who had coined the expression. He and the Reverend Benton Pixley and their followers subscribed to the philosophy of other champion vendors of falsehood: "Tell a lie, make it big, repeat it often, and the majority of the people will believe you."[83]

Avery Campbell handed me another excerpt from a Henry Baum article. Reporting on the demand made of the Mormon leaders that they take but fifteen minutes to evacuate the entire Church membership from Independence, Baum had written:

"[The committee] called on Mr. Phelps, the editor of the *Star;* Edward Partridge, the bishop of the sect; and Mr. Gilbert, the keeper of the church's storehouse; and some others; but they declined any direct answer to the requisition made upon them; and wished an unreasonable stay, in order to consult not only with their brethren here, but in Ohio.

"Whereupon, it was unanimously resolved by the meeting that the *Star* printing office should be razed to the ground, and the type and press secured, which resolution was, with the utmost order and the least noise and disturbance possible, forthwith carried into execution, as also some other steps of a similar tendency; but no blood was spilled, nor any blows inflicted."[84]

I refolded the paper and handed it back to Mr. Campbell.

"For years I thought Lieutenant Governor Boggs was a good man," I said, quietly. "He was rising in prominence in the state; I wanted to rise with him. Certainly, I knew he was ambitious, but I never suspected him capable of treachery. As for the reports from Independence, I knew the leaders of the opposition to the Saints were impassioned, but I had no reason to disbelieve their claims against the Mormons. Well-respected men, religious men, such as Reverend Pixley, were the ones making the allegations. And when Phelps's printing office was destroyed, I understood the action to be legal, by mandate.

"Then the reports started coming in: rumors of mobocracy, people being burned out, beaten, raped. After a time, I realized I'd been duped, so I went to Independence to see for myself. After I had witnessed the reality of the situation, I never wrote under the name of Henry Baum again."

"That's not entirely accurate, is it?" Mr. Campbell challenged me. I viewed him quizzically. "I didn't know until this morning," he stated, "that Henry Baum wrote once more, to denounce Boggs's support of religious intolerance and rule by mob."[85]

Again, I was astounded by my colleague's ability as a researcher. "Too little, too late, I'm afraid," I said. "The damage was done. It's not a time in my career I'm proud of. I made a terrible mistake, which I am sure hurt many of your people. I have regretted my role as a supporter of the mobocrats."

"As well you should," Mr. Campbell agreed.

"Yes?"

"Mine was one of the houses burned to the ground. My eight-year-old boy kicked one of the mobbers in the shin as we were being forced from our home. The brute hit my son in the head with the butt of his rifle and left him bleeding in the dirt. My wife and I tended to him, but he was never the same. He never spoke again; he just sat in a silent stupor. Two years later, while we were living in Clay County, he had a seizure and died—not quite ten. On our gate, the mob had nailed a quote from Henry Baum's article: 'The Mormons are the common enemies of mankind and ought to be destroyed.'"[86]

I felt my eyes fill and looked away. I sensed Mr. Campbell rise and step behind me. After a moment, he rested his hand on my shoulder. "Why didn't you expose me?" I whispered.

"I thought about it for a long while—even had all the documents gathered, all except the one I found this morning—Henry Baum denouncing Boggs. Yesterday, when I saw how much William respected you, I decided to wait. I knew you came here to get an article against Joseph Smith. But as I observed you, I sensed your approach to be fair. Perhaps, I thought to myself, this man has had a change of heart. Maybe when he hears all of William's story he will go easy on him. As for me, I've turned the incident over to God. I've had some feelings—bitter feelings—that I'm not proud of. When you came I could hardly bear to look at you. I'd be lying if I told you otherwise. But I'm over that resentment now and sorry for how I've felt. I would be proud to call you friend. I guess I'd like to forget and be forgiven of some of the things I've done."

We remained quiet with his hand resting on my shoulder for a long time. Only when Waterman Phelps found us did Mr. Campbell and I speak again.

CHAPTER 7

WATERMAN WAS PUFFING AS HE hurried toward us. I supposed by his hurried gait that he intended to continue the tongue lashing he had begun at his father's house. I remained seated and looked away, still trying to absorb Avery Campbell's revelation. I assume the reporter waived off Waterman's intention because he paused in front of me as though he were trying to decide what to say. I was shocked when he called me by my first name and extended his hand.

"Can you ever forgive me?" he asked.

I stared up at a sincere face.

"In my eagerness to protect my father, I lost perspective. I know your questions are not meant to injure him, but to clarify difficult points. My father knows this, too. He can be gruff. So can I. That's part of being a Phelps, I suppose. But both my father and I know your heart is good. That is why you were the only journalist he consented to interview him at this time of his life. Will you let me buy you lunch?" He hadn't stopped pumping my hand during his oration.

I glanced with embarrassment at Mr. Campbell—who had insisted that I begin to call him Avery—and he gestured that I accept Waterman's offer. "You're too kind," was all I could say.

"Let me take your hat," Waterman said, when we three had entered a small eatery. I handed it to him along with my cane and coat, and we settled at a table. As we had walked through the streets of Salt Lake City, the two men had sandwiched me between them and had pelted me with information they felt would be valuable in telling William's story.

For example, Avery informed me that around twelve hundred Mormon people were driven from their homes that bitter November of 1833. Their damaged property was valued at $175,000, which included the burning of 203 homes, one grist mill, the destruction of crops, and the loss of livestock and household furnishings.[87]

Waterman described for me a heavenly display that had manifested itself during one night while the Saints were huddled on the muddy banks of the Missouri River. He said thousands of bright meteors had shot across the sky, trailing long tails of light in their wake. He quoted Parley P. Pratt's description of that night: "It seemed that every star in the broad expanse had been suddenly hurled from its decreed course, and sent lawless through the wilds of ether."[88] The fiery display went on for hours, filling the mob with awe and sending them in fear to their homes.

Waterman told me that the phenomenon was taken by the distressed Saints as a sign of heavenly deliverance.[89]

As we lunched on beef stew and corn bread, Avery shared with me a poem William Phelps had penned as the refugees fled to the banks of the Missouri River in a driving November rain. He called it "Now Let Us Rejoice in the Day of Salvation."[90] I commented that I knew something of William's talents as a reporter and orator, but I did not know of his gift as a poet.

"Many of my father's verses were put to music and sung as hymns," Waterman said, searching through his satchel and producing a Mormon hymnal. He named several of the hymns Phelps had written. I read the words. The impassioned lines articulated the essence of Mormonism—the hope, the vision, the glory of the latter-day work. William's poetry also described the Church's doctrines: the rolling out of the kingdom of God, the restoration of power, the promise of the Savior's return, and the establishment of Zion. William had written of former truths restored, ancient societies revisited, the future of the human family, and the Fatherhood of God. He had taken the teachings of Joseph Smith and made them sing.

I took particular interest in William's lyric entitled "Adam-ondi-Ahman," which Mr. Quinney had earlier boasted he had sung thither and yon. Avery coached me on the spelling of the peculiar place-name and sounded it out for me, stating that it was a phrase carried over from the pure Adamic language into English, one for which there had been no revealed, literal translation. But, as nearly as could be judged, he said, it meant the place or land of God where Adam dwelt.[91] Although I had not visited that area of Missouri, I knew by description the part of the state where Adam-ondi-Ahman was said to be located.

I was told of Joseph Smith's prophecy that the area was the place where Adam would come to visit his people in the latter days and hold a great council as a prelude to the coming of the Lord. Joseph had taught that the valley had been the setting for a similar council held some 5,000 years earlier when Adam, then 927 years old and just three years away from his death, called together his righteous children and gave them his final blessing, prophesying all that would happen to his posterity in all generations. It was there the Savior appeared and blessed Adam, calling him Michael the Archangel.[92] William's lyric spoke of an utopian society that had existed in Adam-ondi-Ahman, possibly providing a model for Enoch's Zion, one in which men lived holy lives, having all things in common and worshiping Jesus face to face. I was told that the hymn had become a favorite of the early Church and had been sung on such special occasions as the dedication of the Kirtland Temple.[93]

Waterman informed me that his father had penned many lyrics for hymns while assisting Emma

Smith in her compilation of a hymnbook for the Church.[94] In fact, twenty-six of the original ninety texts that appeared in that first volume were written or adapted by William W. Phelps.[95] Over time, several had become mainstays and were frequently sung in Mormon worship services. William's pen had indeed been the pen of the Restoration.

Avery and Waterman gave me a brief tour of some of William's better-known lyrics. In addition to "Now Let Us Rejoice" and "Adam-ondi-Ahman," the two men pointed out: "Redeemer of Israel," "Praise to the Man," "Glorious Things Are Sung of Zion," "Gently Raise the Sacred Strain," "O God, the Eternal Father," "The Spirit of God," and "If You Could Hie to Kolob," a text from William's poem entitled "Eternalism," which he had written for Brigham Young.[96] Avery informed me that "hie" means "to hasten," which I was grateful to learn.

These texts, my companions explained, along with William's others, grew out of an uncommon understanding of the gospel of Jesus Christ, a longing for Zion, and a grasping of the events that had been part of the unfolding of a glorious restoration of all things with attendant heavenly manifestations and powers. It was all somewhat overwhelming, but Avery and Waterman spoke with such feeling of these things that I began to appreciate the feeling of fire William's inspired words had generated in the Latter-day Saints. His view was not narrow. He wrote of eternity, of God's dwelling place, the immensity of space, and the endless possibilities of the human soul. All these things, Avery pointed out, indicated William's intimacy with the teachings of the Prophet Joseph.

Waterman was anxious to have me know that his father drew much of what he wrote from the scriptures and cited such phrases as "Our shadow by day and our pillar by night"; "why in the valley of death should they weep?"; and "the tokens already appear" as typical of William's familiarity with holy writ. When he drew my attention to one particular passage, it occurred to me that greater praise has never been put to paper than: "He looks! and ten thousands of angels rejoice, and myriads wait for his word; He speaks! and eternity, Filled with his voice, Re-echoes the praise of the Lord."[97]

In recounting his father's life, Waterman summed up an eventful time: "The year 1836 had dawned in hope. The Missouri Saints were temporarily safe in Clay County, and Joseph was preparing to translate the Book of Abraham from ancient Egyptian papyri. My father was to be one of Joseph's scribes for the Book of Abraham translation, and, of course, the Church was readying itself for one of the most significant events of this dispensation: the dedication of the Kirtland Temple."[98]

"I attended the dedication," Avery said. "I came up from Missouri." He recalled that the congregation sang three of William's hymns on that occasion. "Adam-ondi-Ahman," "Now Let Us Rejoice," and "The Spirit of God."[99] At the mention of that last hymn, Waterman offered this observation: "Immediately following the dedicatory prayer, the congregation sang 'The Spirit of God.' President Smith had been so taken with the hymn that he had asked that the words be written on white satin and displayed before the people.[100] Incredible manifestations of the Spirit accompanied the dedication.

"In its chorus, the hymn encompasses the ancient Hosanna Shout." He then quoted it: "'Hosanna, hosanna to God and the Lamb!'[101] We in the assembly repeated that phrase together, waving white handkerchiefs while doing so." Avery added that the pattern had been revealed to Joseph and was the same practiced by the ancient Israelites in their ceremonies and feasts.[102]

Waterman produced from his satchel an account Joseph Smith had written describing the events: "A noise was heard like the sound of a rushing mighty wind, which filled the Temple, and all the congregation simultaneously arose, being moved upon by an invisible power; many began to speak in tongues and prophesy; others saw glorious visions; and I beheld the Temple was filled with angels. . . . The people of the neighborhood came running together (hearing an unusual sound within, and seeing a bright light like a pillar of fire resting upon the Temple), and were astonished at what was taking place."[103]

"Truly," remarked William's son, "the people sang and shouted with the armies of heaven."

I scratched notes as Waterman and Avery talked. My head was spinning with more than I could write when Mr. Campbell said, "You still don't know who William Phelps is, do you?"

I beckoned him to look at my notebook bulging with data about the man. He told me that my pages were as leaves on trees. What was the root of the man? I was challenged. Who was William Phelps, really? Did I understand his importance to the kingdom and to Joseph personally? I admitted that my bits and pieces had not yet formed a full portrait of the man. But, I questioned, was that the purpose of this interview? I reminded my colleague that William's history and that of the early Church was interesting, but my publisher had sent me to Salt Lake for William's last statement about Joseph, and that was something for which I was still waiting.

"And you shall have it," Waterman interjected, "but please allow my father to tell it in his own way. He has lived life at extremes—on the one hand as one of the Prophet's most trusted friends, on the other as one of Joseph's and the Church's most bitter enemies. None of this is easy for him," his son reminded me, "but hear him out. There is something in my father's story that you and the entire world should know about Joseph Smith, something that is seldom preached from the pulpit, something that could easily die with my father."

Of course, I was intrigued. We said little as we strolled back to William's house and paused before going inside. I turned to Avery Campbell. "You were saying I should become familiar with the 'root' of the man."

The reporter produced a handkerchief from his pocket and wiped his glistening face. I followed his lead and removed my suit coat and loosened my tie. "Let me fill in a few blank spots, sir," he said.

"Shall I take notes?"

"If you wish."

I sat on one of the front steps, while Avery leaned against the railing and Waterman claimed a step below me.

Avery began. "In addition to William Phelps's acting as a scribe for the Prophet's translation of the Book of Abraham, he also assisted in compiling the Doctrine and Covenants.[104] William was in the enviable position of having Joseph Smith explain to him the revelations of God, the coming forth of the Restoration, the future of the kingdom, and the Second Coming of the Lord. He enjoyed fellowship with the Prophet and was tutored by him in spiritual matters, in a way that few others were. Moreover, when Joseph ran for president of the United States, William helped draft his platform and author correspondence to the nations in Joseph's behalf.[105] William was also central in writing the Prophet's history.[106] He served Joseph as mayor's clerk in Nauvoo and was even the fire warden there. Although he was never numbered with them, William often met in council with the Twelve Apostles.[107] After he arrived in Utah, he was elected to the Legislative Assembly of the Territory of Deseret and later became Speaker of the House. He helped write the constitution of the state of Deseret and was also appointed a member of the Board of Regents of the University of Deseret and was admitted to the bar in 1851."[108]

"Interesting," I responded, "but just more details."

"I wanted to broaden your appreciation for the man."

"And you have," I agreed, "but make your point about the 'root' of William Phelps. What is it you want me to discover?"

Avery thought a moment. "You may be right," he stated finally, in a resigned tone. His quick admission of defeat startled me. "The sum of William Phelps's life is the aggregate of the parts. Maybe I cannot verbalize well what I hope you will see in the man. Let me say this, though, and please understand that this is my opinion: William Wines Phelps was as important to the Restoration as any man who lived. Few knew or loved the Prophet as well as he. Few had the responsibility of interpreting the founding events of the Restoration and recording the Prophet's words and deeds as did William. In nearly every page of early Church records and publications, one can see William's pen, his genius." Avery paused. "I make these points so that you will be patient with what you will hear this afternoon. Then, you will have to make your own determination: Who is W. W. Phelps? And who was Joseph Smith, the man William sustained as the prophet of God and whom he loved as a brother? You know by now that William has his own agenda for this interview. It has nothing to do with Church history or his own accomplishments. I believe he is filling you with background so that you will understand the weight of what he has to say. I beg you, let him do so. The fact that he has allowed you this interview shows his trust in your editorial fairness. I leave to you, sir, the task of final judgment."

I closed my notebook. My burden had increased. With my two companions, I stepped back inside William's adobe house at Old Fort, into what was to prove the most thought-provoking afternoon of my life.

CHAPTER 8

A FAIR QUESTION, MR. TALESFORD," William began.
"My companions and I had entered his room and
hadn't yet taken our seats when he made his statement.

"Pardon?" I moved a chair under me and fumbled
for my notebook.

"You inquired why Joseph Smith had left us alone
in Missouri, to be driven and killed, while he
remained presumably safe from harm's way in Ohio."

"Are you sure you want to continue?" I asked. His
nod told me yes. Waterman and Avery had traded
chairs. I could see that William's bed linen had been
changed, his medicines reorganized on the small
table at the side of his bed, and his water glass
refilled, evidences of the loving hands that attended
him. He seemed more frail and perhaps a bit more
pale. His voice sounded weaker, too, yet animated.
I glanced at Waterman for permission to start. He
nodded.

"I meant no offense by my question concerning

Joseph's whereabouts, Mr. Phelps," I confessed. "Perhaps you can enlighten me."

"Of course," he replied. "Thank you for allowing me a little passion in my narrative. And the name's William," he reminded me, smiling.

"Joseph was ever forward-looking.[109] He had the ability to move ahead and remain focused in spite of setbacks. His capacity for work was unmatched Joseph seemed on a dead run to accomplish what the Lord had laid out as his mission. That is not to say that he hadn't time for individuals. Somehow, his faculties expanded as needs presented themselves, and his charity was as broad as eternity. You must understand that Joseph had been tutored by the Lord and possessed a distinct style of administration. As President, he assigned stewardships, taught correct principles, and trusted us to minister to our assigned flocks. I served in the Church presidency in Missouri. Not once did Joseph usurp that presidency's authority. Still, he held us accountable.

"But let me help you understand some of the defining highlights of Joseph's year in Ohio in 1833 In January, he established the School of the Prophets and became its instructor. In February, he finished the translation of the New Testament and received the Lord's law of health, the Word of Wisdom. In March, he organized the First Presidency and expanded the Church organization in Missouri to include me and six other elders. By June, work had started on the Kirtland Temple. Also in June, he finished the plat for the city of New Jerusalem to be built in Missouri. In July, Joseph completed his translation of the entire Bible. In August, he received a revelation from God that a temple should be built with all haste in the land of Zion. By December, Joseph had established the printing office in Kirtland and begun publishing *The Evening and Morning Star*, with Oliver Cowdery. In the midst of court battles and severe persecution, a constant flow of converts was arriving in Kirtland. Building Kirtland as a stronghold for the Church became one of his primary focuses. I hope you can see, Mr. Talesford, that the Prophet had plenty to do at Church headquarters in Ohio, and he allowed us, as leaders in Missouri, to handle local affairs as we saw fit.[110] Now, your query about the Prophet's whereabouts raises in me a certain ire since many Saints at the time asked the same, not as a question, but as an accusation. That spirit of criticism was instrumental in bringing down Zion."[111]

"How so?" I asked.

"We were promised that if we would be obedient to the Prophet's command to build the temple in Zion, we would prosper, and Zion would spread itself and become glorious. But we were also cautioned that if we were lax in complying with this commandment the Lord would visit Zion with affliction, and with pestilence, plague, sword, vengeance, and devouring fire. We leaders in Missouri met and discussed Joseph's admonitions, but there the matter ended. Let me just say that we leaders and the people gave inadequate attention to this revelation.[112] Joseph had taught us that Zion, by definition, is the pure in heart, and many of us tried to live up to that ideal. However, some were disappointed that the Prophet had not moved his residence to Missouri. Some leaders harbored jealousies of the brethren in Ohio who enjoyed the constant companionship of the Prophet.[113] As I mentioned earlier, Zion was awash in bickering, faultfinding, and insinuation. I have told you of President Smith's rebuke to the Missouri Saints and his call to repentance."

I wrote as fast as the words fell from William's mouth. I held up a hand, gesturing him to pause a moment as I caught up. The room was silent, except for the scratching of my pencil. I skimmed over my pages of notes until I located the point of my question. "Ah, yes," I said, looking up at William. "When your son and Mr. Campbell took me to lunch today, they shared with me some of your beautiful lyrics. Will you allow me to digress a moment?" William motioned yes.

"They introduced me to one text with which I was especially intrigued: 'Now Let Us Rejoice in the Day of Salvation.' Did you not pen that lyric during the period you are now describing?"

"You are a musician?" asked William, seemingly amused.

"I am an appreciator more than a participant," I confessed. "Although as a boy I once made an attempt at the clarinet; I never could get used to the reed. I'm afraid I disgraced the instrument. I laid it mercifully aside many years ago."

William found my dramatic recounting humorous. "Well, I don't compose music, but I love to write verse," he said. "Sometimes a talented soul has married my lyric to a tune. Other times I have found a melody that fits my words."[114] He let that idea linger a moment. "All right," he resigned, "I'll tell you about 'Now Let Us Rejoice,' but I won't sing it for you."

"Fair enough," I answered, and I settled back into my chair.

"I've already described the mobbings that went on in Missouri during the fall of 1833," he began. "Property was destroyed, people driven from their homes, and members of the Church assaulted."

William asked his son for more water, then continued. "On November 5th, the mob sent runners throughout Jackson County with false stories that the Mormons had been joined by the Indians, had taken the village of Independence, and had gone to Wilson's store and shot his son. All through that night the mob gathered firearms in preparation for massacring the Saints the next day. The disreputable lieutenant governor of the state of Missouri, Lilburn W. Boggs, stood with the mob and participated in their preparations. Under an agreement with Boggs, who, by the way, had sworn on his honor that the Saints could return to their homes and receive no more molestation, the Mormons surrendered their firearms to the state militia, which was in reality the mob.

"Then, the following day, bands of armed men broke their agreement of peace and attacked the Saints, bursting into houses without fear of armed resistance, frightening women and children with the warning to leave by nightfall or their houses would be torn down and they would be massacred.

"All during the days of November 5th and 6th, the Saints fled in all directions from the merciless mob. On Thursday, November 7th, the banks of the Missouri River were lined on both sides with Mormon exiles. Our sudden flight left families separated—husbands hunting for wives, wives searching for husbands, parents inquiring after their children. As soon as we could, some of us gathered our families and some possessions and crossed the river by ferry into Clay County. There, we constructed makeshift shelters to protect ourselves from the cold rain and sleet that poured down in torrents. In this terrible condition—defeated and defenseless— a spark of hope settled on my mind, and I wrote the lyric to which you have referred. I called it 'Now Let Us Rejoice in the Day of Salvation.'"[115]

William requested that his son and Mr. Campbell sing it for me. Avery shrank from the request, claiming tone deafness, and Waterman suddenly developed a respiratory problem. I was thus spared their singing the hymn but later copied these remarkable words from the Mormon hymnal:

Now let us rejoice in the day of salvation.
No longer as strangers on earth need we roam.
Good tidings are sounding to us and each nation,
And shortly the hour of redemption will come,
When all that was promised the Saints will be given,
And none will molest them from morn until ev'n,
And earth will appear as the Garden of Eden,
And Jesus will say to all Israel, "Come home."

We'll love one another and never dissemble,
But cease to do evil and ever be one.
And when the ungodly are fearing and tremble,
We'll watch for the day when the Savior will come,
When all that was promised the Saints will be given,
And none will molest them from morn until ev'n,
And earth will appear as the Garden of Eden,
And Jesus will say to all Israel, "Come home."

In faith we'll rely on the arm of Jehovah
To guide thru these last days of trouble and
    gloom,
And after the scourges and harvest are over,
We'll rise with the just when the Savior doth
    come.
Then all that was promised the Saints will be
    given,
And they will be crown'd with the angels of
    heav'n,
And earth will appear as the Garden of Eden,
And Christ and his people will ever be one.[116]

CHAPTER 9

A LONG SILENCE SETTLED ON William's room. A restless Waterman followed the progress of a fly dumbly throwing itself against the windowpane. Avery Campbell sought the shock of hair at his forehead. William searched the ceiling, and I waited. At length, without turning to look at me, William said, "And that's when my troubles began. . . ."

For the next quarter hour, he rehearsed the events that had led Joseph Smith to flee Kirtland. There had been a plot hatched by his enemies to take the Prophet's life, but Joseph fled the assassins' hands and with his family made his way to Far West, Missouri. Back in Kirtland, the few remaining loyal Saints vacated the city as fast as preparations could be made. A terrible spirit of apostasy had gripped the city, and some of Joseph's closest associates and Church leaders had turned against him.[117] Brigham Young later stated that at the height of the Ohio apostasy, there could be found no more than twenty persons in Kirtland who would declare Joseph a prophet.[118] Due to a threat on his own life, Brigham Young also fled Kirtland, on December 22nd. Apostates took control of the temple in early January of 1838.[119]

William reported what had led to such dire circumstances. April and May of 1837 were boom days for Kirtland. But financial disaster struck the United States in May and raged through every region. Land values plummeted. Across the nation, eight hundred banks with assets of one hundred twenty million dollars collapsed in a single month. The country was thrown into the worst depression it had known since its birth. The Kirtland Safety Society had been established because the Church's petition to charter a bank in Kirtland had been denied. The Safety Society was intended to provide many of the services of a bank and make loans available to the Church and its members. William stated that the institution might have weathered the financial storm, which enveloped the nation, had it not been for the malfeasance and thievery of some of the management.

The spirit of speculation had taken root in Kirtland as it had throughout the United States. Huge profits were made in short periods of time. Almost everyone was determined to become rich. Humility and faithfulness to duty had been replaced by pride, greed, faultfinding, and dissension.[120] In the frenzied pursuit of wealth, some of the Safety Society's officers, without the knowledge of Sidney

Rigdon, the president, and Joseph Smith, the treasurer, took out one hundred thousand dollars to purchase farms, wagons, and livestock. Managers of the Safety Society took deposits and gave the money to gamblers and speculators to purchase more property. A teller, Warren Parish, admitted to taking $20,000 from the vault. Two of the Twelve, Apostles Lyman E. Johnson and John F. Boynton, took thousands of dollars to New York City where they purchased merchandise to set up a store.

Brigham Young was the first to discover the embezzlement and misappropriations. Joseph spoke out against the hog-wild greed and speculation, which had become obsessions in Kirtland. His words were ignored and knowing that this serious situation threatened the very existence of the Church, Joseph resigned from the Safety Society, disposed of his holdings, and disassociated himself from the establishment. But when the economic fabric in Kirtland began to unravel, the finger of blame was pointed at Joseph, whom many began calling a fallen prophet, one who claimed to have the ear of God yet had led them into financial ruin. William instructed me that these complainers were the ones who had not heeded Joseph's counsel, but now they shackled him with the responsibility for their reckless deal-makings. He told me that Brigham Young later spoke of the crisis in Kirtland as a time when earth and hell seemed in league to overthrow the Prophet and the Church of

God. "The knees of many of the strongest men in the Church faltered," William quoted Brigham Young as saying.[121]

Stillness filled the room once more as William rested and gathered his thoughts. I almost spoke to encourage him, but Waterman made eye contact with me, indicating I should delay. Feeling my leg tingle again, I stood to stretch it and walked to the window. In the late afternoon, a few clouds had billowed up over the western desert and a little breeze was stirring the trees. The birds seemed to have taken notice and were cutting short their day's work. I thought Salt Lake seemed quieter.

Looking out over the impressive city, I was reminded of an account I had read as a youth of a courageous sea invasion made by a small force of patriots, who fought to regain their country from an occupying enemy. The commander of the invading force made his attempt, knowing that casualties would be sustained by his brave first wave of troops. But he knew that if they could establish a beachhead, his little army could push inland from there, grow in numbers, and eventually conquer the foe. I considered the world I lived in—with all its depravity, inequality, and ignorance—and perceived that an adversary had seized control and was holding the earth captive. I thought of Joseph Smith's vision of Zion and pondered what a difference that ideal society could make to a world otherwise chained in financial inequality, immorality, and ignorance. I gazed on Salt Lake City and imagined it a beachhead, established after severe defeats. I tried to project into the future and was able to perceive a wave of change beginning at this place, sweeping over the earth, consuming the opposing force and finally taking the kingdom back from the enemy.

William's voice brought me back to my seat. "That spirit of speculation and greediness had spread to Missouri." He measured his words. "I was caught up in it. John Whitmer and I had surveyed the area of Far West several years before and had recommended it as a place of gathering for the Church."[122] Waterman knew his father's sign that he wanted a sip of water. Avery motioned me to patience. After drinking, William continued. "John and I assumed the responsibility for distributing the property in Far West to the Saints as they arrived. The northern half of Far West was recorded in my name and the southern half in John's."[123]

I could see a conflict of interest developing: John Whitmer and William Phelps were members of the Church presidency in Missouri. Occupying positions of authority, they commanded the loyalty of the Saints. I anticipated but feared what William would say next.

"John and I began to distribute the land independently of the High Council," William continued. "We became proud. We had found a way to enrich ourselves at the expense of the poor members of the Church. We used Church funds and the members' money to make a profit."[124]

William said that while Joseph was struggling to preserve the Church in Kirtland, a Church council was held on April 5, 1837, in Missouri, to investigate his behavior and that of John Whitmer. That resulted in Bishop Edward Partridge's taking over the responsibility for the distribution of Church properties.[125]

William read to me a revelation given to the Prophet Joseph Smith on September 4, 1837, in which the Lord chastened the two men: "'Verily thus saith the Lord unto you my servant Joseph—my servants John Whitmer and William W. Phelps have done those things which are not pleasing in my sight, therefore if they repent not they shall be removed out of their places. Amen.'"[126]

William continued: "At the end of 1837, the Prophet himself traveled to Far West and held a conference in which he offered the Missouri Saints an opportunity to sustain John and me as their leaders. At that November 7th meeting, a list of charges was read regarding the two of us. John Whitmer's name was read first, and some objections were made to his leadership. Whereupon, he stood before the assembly and spoke a few words by way of confession. The vote to retain him in the presidency then carried unanimously. After an adjournment, my name was presented. I also spoke to the subject of the charges and offered a confession, following which the congregation sustained me."[127]

But, William admitted, public confession didn't put an end to his and John Whitmer's covetous behavior. Continuing to overstep their authority and to take advantage of their positions resulted in another council held on February 5, 1838. At that meeting, the two leaders were stripped of their callings in the presidency of the Church in Missouri. On March 10th, during another council, which they refused to attend, William Phelps and John Whitmer were tried for persisting in unchristian conduct. The council decreed that they "be no longer members of the Church of Christ of Latter-day Saints, and be given over to the buffetings of Satan, until they learn to blaspheme no more against the authorities of God, nor fleece the flock of Christ."[128] William was careful to quote the words of the denunciation accurately.

A pause in William's recital gave me an opportunity to scratch a few more notes. I looked at Waterman and Avery, whose expressions spoke their hope for my discretion. I gazed at William, who had turned his head and seemed to be resting. I felt uncomfortable. I straightened in my chair. Maybe if I stood and paced, I thought. It helped a little. Finally, I cleared my throat and, in a soft voice, ventured a question.

"Why, William?" I asked. "Why did you turn? Whatever was in your mind?"

I turned away from him so he wouldn't have to look at me when he answered. I faced instead Waterman and Avery, who alternated between looking at me and past me to William. I detected no rebuke in their countenances. They had permitted me to venture a difficult question but quiet hung heavy in the room. Finding the silence oppressive, I had resolved to amend my query when William finally spoke.

"I don't know," he said. "That's not to say I was not in full control of my faculties—I certainly was cognizant of my actions. For me, that was a time of unbridled rationalization—you remember: 'Tell a lie, make it big, repeat it often, and the majority of the people will believe you.'" I glanced at Avery, who stared at me impassively. "A little sin, rationalized and unchecked, will eventually grow out of control until it chokes and destroys its host," William said. "I had pride and greed hidden in me. It was discovered and exploited by Satan. I soothed myself, justified my pride, minimized my greed, excused my sin." He paused. "I have asked myself over and over again how I could have let it happen. I've tried to understand how I could have let myself become so hardened, so distant, so dark. That I don't know how it happened is the most frightening part. I can only conclude that it can happen to anyone who is not careful."

I paced in silence, finding nothing to add. I thought of a failed marriage and a five-year-old girl in tears. Did I know how *that* happened? Not completely. But, the regret was as alive as William's and had been for many years. Some small fault in me had also been detected by an enemy and exploited, as William had stated. I could no longer draw upon the rationalizations I had conjured at that time. I might have tried to excuse myself, but who would hear me? A malignancy had taken root in me, and I had ignored the signs of its growth.

I took my seat as William began to relate the events that followed. "Once excommunicated, John Whitmer and I began to fight against the Saints, stirring up opposition, urging lawsuits, spreading rumors, publishing slanderous reports, and generally fueling the anger of the mobs.[129] On July 8th 1838, the Lord, through a revelation given to the Prophet, gave me a chance to repent. But I refused.[130] I continued my public venting, and on October 27th, Governor Boggs issued his extermination order, demanding that all Mormons leave the state or be killed.[131] My vicious writings had given the governor additional ammunition for his deadly mandate.[132] On that order, mobs and militia combined to drive out or destroy the Mormons. I had used the great talent God had given me for the building up of His kingdom to destroy it instead. I am good at what I do, Mr. Talesford. Either for good or for evil, I can wield a pen as few in this generation. And God also gave me a gift of oration. When I speak, I am believed. But, I used my gifts against God, His people, and His prophet.

That was when your newspaper first quoted me.[133] As a pro-Mormon writer, I had never received the *Examiner's* attention. But as a dissident, a newly excommunicated member of the Church, one who had the goods on 'ol' Joe Smith,' as journalists loved to call him, I was anxiously sought after for interviews and given prime space for my angry words and lies."

I interrupted the old man, who seemed bent on taking full blame for the travesties of that time. "I understand that you turned against the Church and your former associates," I noted, "but don't you think you are being a bit hard on yourself?" I didn't wait for his reply. "After all, persecutions existed before your leaving the Church—harsh persecutions. Certainly Governor Boggs's determination to wipe Missouri clean of the Mormons was not a recent idea. I knew him. For years he had been looking for an excuse to rid the state of Mormons. How can you suggest your role was central to those dire happenings?"

"I will not pardon myself, sir!" he returned forcibly. "Neither you nor anyone can soften what I did and who I became. Believe me, I tried for nearly two years to justify my position."[134] He spoke with greater feeling. "I will not absolve myself. What I did, I did with my eyes open. I calculated my revenge and actively campaigned against the people of God and the Prophet. Did I cause all the troubles? No, it would be vain to say so. But I contributed. Governor Boggs issued his extermination order, and I applauded."

William closed his eyes and held a bony hand to his forehead as he spoke. "The massacre at Haun's Mill resulted from Boggs's order.[135] Nineteen men and boys were slaughtered in that inhuman raid; one boy was only seven years of age!"

He continued. "Do you want to know my recurring nightmare?" He went on without my responding. "Another boy, Sardius Smith, was just ten. He was dragged from his hiding place by a Mr. Glaze, who placed the muzzle of his gun to the boy's head while the little lad begged for his life. Without thought, the butcher shot the top of the boy's head off saying, 'Nits make lice, and if he had lived he would have become a Mormon.'"[136] William's voice broke, and he paused to gain control of his emotions. At length, he said, "My words had helped fuel that mob's hatred."

William blinked back his tears and drew a ragged breath before continuing. "The Prophet was captured and condemned to be executed at the public square at Far West. Thanks to Alexander Doniphan, the commander who refused to carry out the order, the Prophet's life was spared.[137] Still, I had contributed to the Prophet's near death."

William coughed, and Waterman moved quickly to his side, assuring him he did not have to go on. The old man shook his head but allowed his son to hold him until he resumed breathing normally. After a time, Waterman laid him gently back on his pillow. Only then did I speak. "William, I fear this interview has gone on too long. I can return tomorrow or withdraw altogether, if that is your wish."

William shook his head again. "I know where I am headed in the next few days. Nothing can stop that. But you, sir, will hear my story—all of it. You have come here to discover if Joseph is my friend and whether I will defend or renounce him on my deathbed. You shall presently hear. Please indulge me a little longer."

I reluctantly opened my book of notes. I would be as quiet as possible for the remainder of what William had to say. But I was feeling something that disturbed me. As a journalist, I had known many of the defining moments of Missouri's history, but I had allowed myself little emotional involvement. That I was feeling anything close to empathy in that adobe house in Old Fort came as an uncomfortable shock. I felt in danger of losing the impartiality I had been careful to cultivate. But then I thought, could anyone, no matter how hardened, not feel some pathos for such a story?

"I was one of those who betrayed Joseph to the mob," William said. "The mob called themselves the state militia. They surrounded Far West, outnumbering the Mormons five to one. They demanded that the Prophet and other Mormon leaders surrender. Joseph did not know that Colonel Hinkle, one of his most trusted men, who also led the Mormon Far West Militia, had made a secret arrangement with the Prophet's enemies to deliver Joseph and other

Mormon leaders into the mob's hands for trial. Many have said Colonel Hinkle acted out of fear of the impending massacre. Historians will have to decide. As for me, I aided Colonel Hinkle; I consented to and backed the betrayal.

"In addition to delivering up the Prophet to the mob, Hinkle and I suggested that the property of the Mormons, who had taken up arms to defend themselves, should be confiscated to pay for debts and damages resulting from the mob's actions. We connived that the Saints would give up their arms of every description in exchange for receipts, and that all the Saints would leave the state under the pretense of protection by the very militia that was threatening them. Toward evening, we put our plan in motion by having Colonel Hinkle come to Joseph with the lie that the heads of the state militia wished to interview him. When Joseph, Hyrum, and others showed up at the militia's camp to discuss peace, they were taken as prisoners of war and treated with utmost contempt.[138] I was a Judas, don't you see? When the Prophet was tried in court, I testified against him. I wrote a condemning affidavit to the court, and I signed it. It was used against Joseph at his trial." William asked his son to locate and give me the statement, which Waterman reluctantly did.

I read the document in silence. William had sworn in his affidavit that secret meetings had been held among Church leaders and others, and that he had endeavored to find out what those meetings were about. The document declared that William had learned that Joseph and others had formed a secret society called the Danites, the members of which had entered into a covenant that if any Mormon attempted to move out of the county, the Danites would kill him and haul him aside in the brush, and that all the burial he would have would be in a turkey buzzard's guts. Further, if any non-Mormon from the surrounding county came into a Mormon town, walking about—no matter who he might be—any one of the Danites would kill that stranger and throw him aside into the brush.[139]

"From the first instance," William stated, "I attempted to link Joseph to the Danites, a secret society, sworn to murder and plunder in the name of protection for the Saints.[140] The charge against Joseph was, of course, false, and his involvement in the conspiracy of the Danites was contrived—a bald-faced lie."

William next showed me his letter to the Missouri State Legislature, congratulating the behavior of the state militia in its dealings with the Mormons.[141]

"Largely based upon my actions and testimony," said William, "Joseph Smith and others were imprisoned in Liberty Jail. They remained there the four months from November 30th 1838, until April 6th 1839, when the Saints fled to Illinois, leaving tracks of blood in the snow."[142]

Waterman and Mr. Campbell appeared to be

nervous as I copied parts of William's sworn statements into my notebook. William waited for me. When I looked up, he continued.

"I want you to picture Liberty Jail in your mind," he said. "It is an edifice of stone with the prisoners' quarters located in an area partly buried underground. The guards were stationed in the upper room. The jail room measured fourteen feet by fourteen and one-half feet and was six and one-half feet high. Its walls, made of stone and wood, were about four feet thick.[143] Two hundred curiosity-seekers came to witness the incarceration of the Prophet. They were disappointed to see that he looked like a normal man—they expected some sub-human in monstrous form, I suppose, equal to the tales that had circulated about him. Before stepping into the jail, Joseph turned to the gawkers, tipped his hat, and in a cordial manner said, 'Good afternoon, gentlemen.'[144]

"The winter of 1838-39 was reported to have been the coldest on record. The prisoners—Joseph, Hyrum, Sidney Rigdon, Lyman Wight, Alexander McRae, and Caleb Baldwin—could build no fire because the only two narrow, grated slits in the walls, one foot high and two feet wide, provided inadequate ventilation. Those slits, however, allowed the awful cold to seep in and stay. Cold air, as you know, Mr. Talesford, is weighty and will settle and remain if left unheated. Liberty Jail's basement air remained as cold as the coldest day of that winter. Ice, in fact, formed on the walls of the prisoners' cells and didn't melt during those frigid days. Candlelight and what little daylight entered the slits provided the only illumination in the miserable cell. The beds were hewn, white-oak logs. The stone floor was covered with dirty straw. The moisture that collected in the dank chamber made the chill more poignant. Three buckets were provided: one for drinking water, one for washing, and one for human waste. What food was given to the inmates was fit only for the garbage barrel. It was delivered in filthy baskets where chickens had roosted and deposited their droppings. Scraps off the jailers' table were considered supplements to the prisoners' diet. Sometimes, family and friends slipped cakes and bread through the window slits to stave off starvation.[145]

"The inmates became wary of the food brought them by the guards, especially the meat, which was dark in color and referred to by their jailers as 'Mormon beef.' [146] Joseph directed his companions not to consume it, warning it was human flesh, but driven by hunger, Lyman Wight ate a little and became violently ill. Small amounts of poison—not enough to prove lethal—were also added to the other food. Sometimes, after consuming the poison, the prisoners lay on their hard oak beds almost vomiting themselves to death, not caring whether they lived or died. Joseph had always been a large man, muscular, barrel-chested, and weighing about two hundred ten pounds. When he escaped from Liberty Jail four months later he was described as looking emaciated, unkempt, and nearly unrecognizable."[147]

William then emphasized each word: "I helped put him in that hellish place. Joseph Smith, once my dearest friend, suffered in that freezing pit because of my sworn testimony."

The picture William had painted provoked in me the keenest sympathy for those who had been made to suffer such persecutions. As a reporter, I had seen some of the results of the mob's actions with my own eyes. I carried in my mind the vision of a people once more driven from their homes, fleeing for their lives in the dead of winter, leaving behind their beloved leader to a cruel and uncertain fate. To that there had been added reports of virgins and wives being strapped to benches and fallen upon by devilish fiends who ravished them repeatedly in full view of helpless husbands and fathers.[148] The vision included the plaintive cries of children, naked and lost in the bitterness of winter, wailing for dead parents; of houses being pillaged, property destroyed, and meetinghouses desecrated. All this, I could not bear. I reached for my handkerchief but found Avery Campbell offering me his. I excused myself and wished for some other sound to muffle my emotional display.

It was a quarter of an hour before I could write again.

CHAPTER 10

"T̲AKE MY ADVICE, M̲R. T̲ALESFORD," spoke William. "Do not find yourself fighting against God and His anointed servants. It is a hell from which no man can easily climb."

I said I doubted that any man in his right mind would assume to oppose God. William speculated that Jesus Christ would have been no more safe in Missouri in 1838 than he had been in Jerusalem eighteen hundred years earlier. "I have wondered," William said, "if I had lived in those days, would I have been one of those who yelled, 'Crucify him!'?"

My first reaction was to assure him that I could not imagine that coarseness in his character. William stopped me with a glance. "But I put His prophet in prison, didn't I? And didn't I help drive the Lord's people from their homes?"

With the afternoon waning, I knew no amount of effort would divert William from his predetermined agenda. That this was his dying statement was obvious. My role had changed from reporter to scribe. I didn't mind. On my return trip to Kansas City I would gather my notes and try to glean from William's words a story worth reading. For the moment, I was content to sit at his bedside. I turned to a new page in my notebook and waited.

"My family and I suffered in misery from the time I turned against Joseph and the Saints," he began. "I thought I had known hardship before. It was nothing compared to the wrath of God. For all my plans of wealth, I found myself penniless. For all my plans of an easy life, I was constantly sick. I grieved from several disorders, accompanied by chills and fever. My wife, Sally, had the fever, too. My boy Waterman," he continued, pointing at his son, "contracted the fever, ague, and inflammatory dysentery. My daughter Sarah had two or three diseases, plus chills and fever." He went on to describe his family's growing impoverishment and other afflictions suffered by them. He spoke of the mental and spiritual distress he had suffered when he felt the Spirit of the Lord withdraw and leave him alone with his deeds. William said he knew the scriptures as well as anyone and knew the terrible judgments that await those who defy God and persecute his chosen people and prophets. At times, he said, he felt he had gone too far,[149] that he had fought against heaven with the full light of truth shining on him and that no redemption could be made for his damned soul.

"I moved my family to Dayton, Ohio, in early

1840," he recalled. "I had hoped to find work there but had no success.[150] Then, when I had decided to return to the East in search of employment, I was visited by Elders Orson Hyde and John Page, who were passing through Dayton on their way to dedicate the land of Palestine for the return of the Jews.[151]

"Seeing my former brethren again was as a light bursting upon a dark prison. I felt the jail doors crack and the tiniest hope enter. I was deeply repentant when they found me. I had been chastened by the Lord's own hand and felt myself lost, a condemned soul, a citizen of hell itself. There was no rationalization left in me, no soothing of my ego, no justifying of my pride, no minimizing of my greed, no excusing of my sin. I wanted to change and be forgiven but didn't know if I had sinned beyond rescue. I knew what I had done. I had played the scenes over and over again in my mind. I knew what part was mine in the orchestrating of those horrible events, and I felt forsaken by God, left to languish in a state of eternal torment without promise of reprieve. A man trained in words and language, I could not express to the elders the misery I felt and how I longed for forgiveness and peace. But they listened as the servants of Christ they were and offered me hope. They encouraged me to write to the Prophet, who was then residing in Nauvoo, Illinois, and ask him to forgive me. They said they would see that my letter was placed in

Joseph's hands along with their letter of recommendation."[152]

William requested a large book from his son. When he had received it, he leafed through its pages until he found his letter to the Prophet, dated June 29th 1840. I now quote it in its entirety:

> BROTHER JOSEPH:—I am alive, and with the help of God I mean to live still. I am as the prodigal son, though I never doubt or disbelieve the fulness of the Gospel. I have been greatly abused and humbled, and I blessed the God of Israel when I lately read your prophetic blessing on my head, as follows:
>
> "The Lord will chasten him because he taketh honor to himself, and when his soul is greatly humbled he will forsake the evil. Then shall the light of the Lord break upon him as at noonday and in him shall be no darkness."
>
> I have seen the folly of my way, and I tremble at the gulf I have passed. So it is, and why I know not. I prayed and God answered, but what could I do? Says I, "I will repent and live, and ask my old brethren to forgive me, and though they chasten me to death, yet I will die with them, for their God is my God. The least

place with them is enough for me, yea, it is bigger and better than all Babylon." Then I dreamed that I was in a large house with many mansions, with you and Hyrum and Sidney, and when it was said, "Supper must be made ready," by one of the cooks, I saw no meat, but you said there was plenty, and you showed me much, and as good as I ever saw; and while cutting to cook, your heart and mine beat within us, and we took each other's hand and cried for joy, and I awoke and took courage.

I know my situation, you know it, and God knows it, and I want to be saved if my friends will help me. As the captain that was cast away on a desert island; when he got off he went to sea again, and made his fortune the next time, so let my lot be. I have done wrong and I am sorry. The beam is in my own eye. I have not walked along with my friends according to my holy anointing. I ask forgiveness in the name of Jesus Christ of all the Saints, for I will do right, God helping me. I want your fellowship; if you cannot grant that, grant me your peace and friendship, for we are brethren, and our communion used to be sweet, and whenever the Lord brings us together again, I will make all the satisfaction on every point that Saints or God can require. Amen.[153]

"Mr. Talesford," William directed himself to me, "can you imagine what anguish I endured during the month I waited for my letter to arrive in Nauvoo and another month before I received a reply?"

I could not.

"The principles of the gospel I had learned and taught became my only hope. The idea of a forgiving God became my obsession. I pled that it might be true. The Savior's atonement—a sacrifice that I had once believed extended to the furthest depths of human misery—seemed insufficient to rescue my decadent soul. Even so, the hope of the Savior's mercy occupied my every thought. That the Lord Jesus Christ might ransom me was my fervent wish and that Joseph and the Saints of God might forgive me was my desire."

With trembling hand, William took a letter from his book and bade me read it. I could see by the signature that the letter had been composed by Joseph Smith. It was dated July 22nd 1840, and had been dispatched from Nauvoo, Illinois.

Dear Brother Phelps: I must say that it is with no ordinary feelings I endeavor to write a few lines to you in answer to yours of the 29th ultimo; at the same time I am rejoiced at the privilege granted me.

You may in some measure realize what my feelings as well as Elder Rigdon's and Brother Hyrum's were, when we read your letter—truly our hearts were melted into tenderness and compassion when we ascertained your resolves, etc. I can assure you I feel a disposition to act on your case in a manner that will meet the approbation of Jehovah, (whose servant I am), and agreeable to the principles of truth and righteousness which have been revealed; and inasmuch as long-suffering, patience, and mercy have ever characterized the dealing of our Heavenly Father towards the humble and penitent, I feel disposed to copy the example, cherish the same principles, and by so doing be a savior of my fellow men.

It is true, that we have suffered much in consequence of your behavior—the cup of gall, already full enough for mortals to drink, was indeed filled to overflowing when you turned against us. One with whom we had oft taken sweet counsel together, and enjoyed many refreshing seasons from the Lord—"had it been an enemy, we could have borne it." "In the day that thou stoodest on the other side, in the day when strangers carried away captive his forces, and foreigners entered into his gates, and cast lots upon [Far West], even thou wast as one of them; but thou shouldest not have looked on the day of thy brother, in the day that he became a stranger, neither shouldest thou have spoken proudly in the day of distress."

However, the cup has been drunk, the will of our Father has been done, and we are yet alive, for which we thank the Lord. And having been delivered from the hands of wicked men by the mercy of our God, we say it is your privilege to be delivered from the powers of the adversary, be brought into the liberty of God's dear children, and again take your stand among the Saints of the Most High, and by diligence, humility, and love unfeigned, commend yourself to our God, and your God, and to the Church of Jesus Christ.

Believing your confession to be real, and your repentance genuine, I shall be happy once again to give you the right hand of fellowship, and rejoice over the returning prodigal.

Your letter was read to the Saints last

Sunday and an expression of their feeling
was taken, when it was unanimously
Resolved, that W. W. Phelps should be
received into fellowship. Yours as ever,
Joseph Smith, Jun.[154]

William let Joseph's text settle on me and fill me
with the weight of its message. I found myself envi-
sioning once again the wrongs Joseph had suffered,
being betrayed and incarcerated by the word of his
friend, enduring unimaginable oppression. I
struggled to comprehend Joseph's capacity for love
and forgiveness, to place the redemption of a lost soul
over personal pain. Then, I thought of William's letter being read to the body of the Church in Nauvoo.
In that audience I could envision victims of inhuman
cruelty, people who had lost everything, even loved
ones. I could picture children who had cried for slain
parents, maidens and wives who had been ravished,
husbands who had watched their homes and property destroyed, families who had trudged through the
bitter snows of Missouri and Illinois. If I had been
one of them, could I have cast a vote of forgiveness
and agreed to bring William W. Phelps back into fellowship? Yet the vote of the congregation was unani-
mous.

The last lines of Joseph's letter to William made
me choke with emotion. It was written as a couplet:

Come on, dear brother, since the war is past,
For friends at first, are friends again at last.

"My joy was full," William sighed. "I was going home." Then he paused. "I could not gather the funds for my family's journey to Nauvoo for some time. Finally, when we could travel, we did so in abject poverty.[155]

"One evening, as we plodded along the road that led into Nauvoo, Joseph spied me at a distance. He left his dinner and ran to greet me. We fell on each other's necks and embraced and wept."[156]

William turned his head from me. His quiet sobbing told me the interview was over. I wanted to say good-bye, knowing that I would never see my friend again. But good-bye seemed strangely inappropriate. I looked to Avery and to Waterman. They gestured me to follow them outside. I quietly collected my notes and stepped from William's room for the last time.

CHAPTER 11

T HANK YOU FOR COMING, MR. Talesford." Waterman shook my hand. Avery said he hoped that I was leaving with something of importance and that I was not too disappointed for not being able to ask more questions. I regarded Waterman's courteous words and told Avery that my time had been well spent. However, in my mind I knew my publisher would feel otherwise.

As I stood at the door, I could feel a chill in the air. Dark clouds blanketed the sky over Salt Lake City, and I expected the city would suffer with the coming storm. I wrapped myself in my coat and adjusted my hat.

"Would you have a moment, sir?" Waterman stopped me.

"Of course," I replied.

"My father remained Joseph's true friend until the end of the Prophet's life. When my father came to Nauvoo, he resumed his writing for Joseph and the Church. He never owned any property in Nauvoo and barely made enough to support his family. Still, few men living in Nauvoo at that time had a more intimate relationship with the Prophet than did William W. Phelps."[157]

I thanked Waterman and started to leave.

"There is more," Avery said. I waited politely. "William visited Joseph Smith in Carthage Jail early in the morning on the day the Prophet and Hyrum were murdered.[158] Two days later, it was William W. Phelps who delivered the funeral sermon to over ten thousand grieving souls."

Avery Campbell gave me a copy of the eulogy and said I should take it with me. It said in part:

"Was Joseph Smith the friend of gamblers, drunkards, robbers, fornicators, adulterers, liars and hypocrites? No; read his life from Vermont to Carthage Jail, and every line and every act, shines with virtuous principles, and words of wisdom, that warms this heart with a godlike sensation. . . .

"What Joseph knew came natural; . . . he quoted the finer sentiments of morals, divinity, legislation, and laws . . . as if he had learned them from his mother's lap; and though they were original with him, they were always correct. He was a man of God. . . . He came, not in a tempest of wrath, but in the still small voice of Jehovah with full power to restore the holy priesthood; he came, not in the whirlwind of public opinion but in the simple name of Jesus Christ with a love that surpasses understanding. . . . He is dead, but he lives; he is absent from us, but at home in heaven. . . . And yet the spirit whispers, what shall I say of Joseph the seer, cut off from his useful life in the midst of his years? Why, I will say that he has done more in fifteen years, to make the truth plain— open the way of life; and carry glad tidings to the meek . . . than all Christendom has done in fifteen hundred years with money, press, and a hired clergy. . . . Tell the world, and let eternity bear record, that the great name of Joseph Smith will go down to unborn worlds and up to sanctified heavens and gods, with all his shining honors and endless fame as stars in his crown, while the infamy of his persecutors can only be written in their ashes. Well may it be echoed, congratulate the dead that die in the Lord, . . . for they can rest from their labors, and their works shall follow them. . . . It is finished! It is finished! The Saints are free; Jehovah's won the victory, and not a righteous man is lost!"[159]

Waterman handed me a Mormon hymnbook, saying that it was a gift. He had marked a page that I turned to as I thanked him. The hymn was entitled, "Praise to the Man."

"My father grieved without consolation for the loss of his closest associate," he said. "A few weeks after Joseph's death, he authored these words.[160] Most see in these verses the honor given to the universal mission of the Prophet. For my father, they are intimately personal—the man who had communed with

Jehovah was my father's dearest friend, the one who had saved him."

I read the hymn silently.

> Praise to the man who communed with Jehovah!
> Jesus anointed that Prophet and Seer.
> Blessed to open the last dispensation,
> Kings shall extol him, and nations revere.
>
> Praise to his mem'ry, he died as a martyr;
> Honored and blest be his ever great name!
> Long shall his blood, which was shed by assassins,
> Stain Illinois while the earth lauds his fame.
>
> Great is his glory and endless his priesthood.
> Ever and ever the keys he will hold.
> Faithful and true, he will enter his kingdom,
> Crowned in the midst of the prophets of old.
>
> Sacrifice brings forth the blessings of heaven;
> Earth must atone for the blood of that man.
> Wake up the world for the conflict of justice.
> Millions shall know "Brother Joseph" again.
>
> Hail to the Prophet, ascended to heaven!
> Traitors and tyrants now fight him in vain.
> Mingling with Gods, he can plan for his brethren;
> Death cannot conquer the hero again.[161]

◆ ◆ ◆

My return trip to Kansas City has been cold. I have traveled with less colorful companions than those who accompanied my expedition to Utah. Having deposited the other passengers at their appointed destinations, I now ride alone the last hundred miles to Missouri. The weather has improved a little. At our last stop I purchased a newspaper. Buried in an obscure corner lay a small reference to the recent death of prominent Mormon leader, William Wines Phelps. From Waterman's parting words, I knew that William would be laid to rest in the Salt Lake City Cemetery and that the poet had requested that selected stanzas from "If You Could Hie to Kolob" be engraved on his headstone:

> *There is no end to matter;*
> *There is no end to space;*
> *There is no end to spirit;*
> *There is no end to race.*
> *There is no end to glory;*
> *There is no end to love;*
> *There is no end to being;*
> *There is no death above.*[162]

The thought of visiting my editor makes me feel old. Maybe I am. I have given two-thirds of my life to journalism. Yet I can think of nothing I have written that will survive me. William's writings will survive him, though. Of that I am certain. Perhaps my father was right after all: I should have followed in the footsteps of my namesake, Washington Irving. The *Kansas City Examiner* won't terminate me for my inability to produce a scandalous story about the Mormons. I will get my hands slapped and from now on these types of stories will go to younger, more hard-nosed reporters. It doesn't matter, I suppose. I feel as though I've earned a vacation after forty years at the *Examiner*. Places like Independence, Liberty, Far West, Carthage, Nauvoo, and Adam-ondi-Ahman intrigue me now. I think I'll take some time and visit them.

Then, there's a little girl in Pennsylvania whom I haven't seen in thirty-five years. If I showed up, would she love me, call me Daddy, let me be a part of her family? Is there enough charity in Pennsylvania to cover the shortcomings of a young, ambitious father who became an old fool? If I came trudging down a deserted, dirt road one evening, would my daughter leave her supper, run to embrace me, and bring me into her home? I wonder if, as William Phelps, I have a friend anywhere such as Joseph Smith?

NOTES

1. William W. Phelps died 6 March 1872 in Salt Lake City, Utah. The idea of a deathbed interview is purely a fabrication of the author for the purpose of telling this story. In actuality, Phelps lay in a near comatose state the last days of his life, unable to speak to anyone. See *A Book of Mormons*, 209.

2. Both Washington Irving Talesford and the *Kansas City Examiner* are fictitious and are not meant to represent any actual person or publication. The stagecoach driver and the passengers are also fictitious characters.

3. Doctrine and Covenants 57:1–3 (hereinafter D&C); Roberts, B. H., *Missouri Persecutions*, 47–53 (hereinafter *MP*).

4. *Encyclopedia of Mormonism*, Vol. 1, ADAM-ONDI-AHMAN (hereinafter *EM*); *EM*, Vol. 2, GARDEN OF EDEN; *Journal of Discourses* 10:235; cf. 11:336–7 (hereinafter *JD*); *Doctrines of Salvation* 3:74 (hereinafter *DS*).

5. *EM*, Vol. 2, HISTORY OF THE CHURCH.

6. *DS*, 3:193.

7. *MP*, 61.

8. A fictitious statement made for the purposes of story-telling.

9. Cook, Lyndon W. *The Revelations of the Prophet Joseph Smith*, 87 (hereinafter, Cook).

125

10. Avery Campbell is a fictitious person whom the author has assigned the part of a *Deseret News* reporter.

11. Cook, 87.

12. News clippings, Harold B. Lee Library, Brigham Young University, 2 (1844): 331–33, 336–37. Bowen, Walter Dean, *The Versatile W.W. Phelps: Mormon Writer, Educator, and Pioneer,* master's thesis, Brigham Young University [1958], 93 (hereinafter Bowen); *Nauvoo Neighbor,* Vol. 1, No. 111 (June 12, 1844), 255; *History of the Church,* 3:359.

13. Cook, 87.

14. Cook, 87–88.

15. Black, Dean, "Praise to the Man," *Latter-day Digest,* Vol. 2, No. 4., 17–19 (hereinafter, Black).

16. Van Orden, Bruce, *Regional Studies,* New York, "W. W. Phelps," 208–13.

17. Black, 19; Bowen, 27.

18. Barrett, Ivan J., *Joseph Smith and the Restoration,* 125–30 (hereinafter, Barrett).

19. Nibley, Hugh, "What Is Zion? A Distant View," *Approaching Zion,* 25.

20. D&C 55.

21. William Phelps, "Letters of W. W. Phelps," UG&HM 31 (Jan 1940), 26.

22. *Messenger and Advocate* (September 1835) 1:177–78.

23. *Times and Seasons,* Vol. 1, No. 12 (Oct. 1840): 71.

24. D&C 101:1–7; *MP,* 122–23.

25. Cook, 87.

26. D&C 57:11.

27. *MP,* 60.

28. Bowen, 40.

29. Bowen, 43.

30. Roberts, B.H., *The Seventy's Course in Theology*, First Year, 135

31. *EM*, Vol. 2, MORONI, VISITATIONS OF.

32. *MP*, 54-56.

33. Barrett, 112-13.

34. D&C 42:30-34.

35. Psalm 24:1; *MP*, 55-56.

36. D&C 49:20.

37. *MP*, 56.

38. Black, 19.

39. Arrington, Leonard J., "Joseph Smith, Builder of Ideal Communities," edited by Larry C. Porter and Susan Easton Black, *The Prophet Joseph Smith—Essays on the Life and Mission of Joseph Smith*, 118.

40. *MP*, 57.

41. Ibid., 60-61, 69-71.

42. Barrett, 168-69.

43. Ibid., 169.

44. *MP*, 61-68.

45. Clark, James R., *Messages of the First Presidency*, Vol. 4, 250.

46. Thomas Quinney is a fictitious character, but information on such work done on the Salt Lake Temple, the Utah Central Railroad, and the various other projects is taken from *The Salt Lake Temple: A Centennial Book of Remembrance, 1893-1993*.

47. *Hymns of The Church of Jesus Christ of Latter-day Saints*, 1985, no. 49 (hereinafter, *Hymns*).

48. Roberts, B. H., *Outlines of Ecclesiastical History*, 354.

49. *The Salt Lake Temple: A Centennial Book of Remembrance, 1893-1993*, 46.

50. *Historical Atlas of Mormonism*, 44.

51. *The Salt Lake Temple: A Centennial Book of Remembrance, 1893-1993*, 52-54.

52. *MP*, 97.

53. Ibid., 69-72.

54. Ibid., 89.

55. A fictitious statement made for the purpose of story-telling.

56. William Phelps, "Letters of W. W. Phelps," UG&HM 31 (Jan 1940), 26.

57. Ibid.

58. *MP*, 107-110; *Millennial Star*, Vol. 14, 582.

59. Barrett, 187.

60. Some evidence exists that Waterman Phelps was a writer and an orator as was his father, but not nearly as prolific.

61. *MP*, 73.

62. Ibid., 73-75.

63. Ibid., 78-80.

64. Ibid., 82-85.

65. Ibid., 85.

66. Ibid., 85; Bowen, 49.

67. Ibid., 85-86.

68. Ibid., 87; Barrett, 181.

69. Ibid., 88.

70. Ibid., 89-90.

71. Barrett, 175.

72. *MP*, 91.

73. Ibid., 91-94; Barrett, 190.

74. Barrett, 181.

75. Ibid., 181.

76. Ibid., 182-83.

77. Clark, James R., *Messages of the First Presidency,* Vol. 4, 243.

78. *History of the Church,* 3:230-31.

79. *EM,* Vol. 3, SEAGULLS, MIRACLE OF.

80. Henry Baum is the pen name of Washington Irving Talesford, both fictitious characters.

81. *MP,* 91.

82. Smith, Joseph Fielding, *Church History and Modern Revelation,* 2:176.

83. Barrett, 171.

84. Evans, John Henry, *One Hundred Years of Mormonism,* 172; Barrett, 173.

85. This statement is fictitious.

86. This is a fictitious event.

87. Barrett, 187.

88. Ibid.

89. Ibid.

90. Davidson, Karen Lynn, *Our Latter-day Hymns, the Stories and the Messages,* 31-32 (hereinafter, Davidson).

91. For a listing of fifteen hymns by W. W. Phelps, see *Hymns,* 390.

92. Smith, Joseph Fielding, *Answers to Gospel Questions,* 1:12.

93. Smith, Joseph, *Teachings of the Prophet Joseph Smith,* sel. Joseph Fielding Smith, 38 (hereinafter, *Teachings*).

94. Davidson, 78-79.

95. Ibid., 9.

96. Cook, 36.

97. *A Book of Mormons,* 209.

98. Barrett, 257-58.

99. Davidson, 30-32, 78-79.

100. Van Wagoner, Richard and Walker, Steven C.; *BYU Studies,* Vol. 23, No. 1, 5.

101. *History of the Church*, 2:427-28; McConkie, Bruce R., *Mormon Doctrine*, 368.

102. McConkie, Bruce R., *The Promised Messiah*, 428-29.

103. *History of the Church*, 2:427-28.

104. Cook, 87.

105. Bowen, 107-09.

106. Ibid.

107. Ibid.

108. Cook, 88.

109. That Joseph was forever forward-looking is evidenced in many accounts of his tribulations, but especially in his opening the gospel to Great Britain. See Barrett, 272.

110. See associated references in Barrett, 564-65; *MP*, 69-72.

111. *MP*, 67, 122

112. McConkie, Bruce R., *A New Witness for the Articles of Faith*, 60; D&C 97:18-28; Barrett, 166.

113. Barrett, 168.

114. For composers who wrote the music attached to Phelps's lyrics, see attribution on individual hymns, *Hymns*, 390.

115. Barrett, 181-87; Davidson, 31-32.

116. *Hymns*, no. 3.

117. Barrett, 268-82.

118. Ibid., 272.

119. Ibid., 282.

120. Ibid., 268-70.

121. Ibid., 269-70.

122. *EM*, Vol. 2, MISSOURI.

123. Barrett, 293.

124. Ibid., 294.

125. Ibid., 295.

126. *History of the Church*, 2:511.

127. Ibid., 2:523.

128. Ibid., 3:3–5, 6–8; Corrill, John, *History of the Mormons* (1839), 27–28.

129. Bowen, 87; *Times and Seasons*, Vol. 1, No. 6 (April 1840), 15.

130. *History of the Church*, 3:46.

131. Ibid., 3:175.

132. Barrett, 325

133. This is a fictitious statement for the purpose of story-telling.

134. *A Book of Mormons*, 207.

135. The massacre at Haun's Mill took place on Tuesday, 30 October 1838. See *History of the Church*, 3:184.

136. Barrett, 328–32; *MP* 234–37.

137. Ibid., 335–36.

138. Ibid., 334–35; Black, 21.

139. Nibley, Hugh, *BYU Studies*, Vol. 11, No. 4, 391.

140. Barrett, 313–15.

141. *History of the Church*, 3:359.

142. Smith, Joseph Fielding, *Church History and Modern Revelation*, 4:67.

143. Barrett, 354.

144. Two hundred curiosity seekers came to see Joseph imprisoned. See Backman, Milton V. and Cowan, Richard O., *Joseph Smith and the Doctrine and Covenants*, 125.

145. Barrett, 354; *EM*, Vol. 2, LIBERTY JAIL; author's interviews with Liberty Jail missionaries.

146. Ibid., 354.

147. Brickey, Wayne, *Education Week* lecture, 1996, Brigham Young University; see also Gentry, Leland, *A History of the Latter-day Saints in Northern Missouri*

1836-1839, a Ph.D. dissertation, Brigham Young University [1965], 352-401.

148. Barrett, 345-46.

149. Bowen, 96.

150. Ibid., 96-97.

151. *History of the Church*, 4:142.

152. Ibid., 4:141-42.

153. Ibid., 4:142.

154. Ibid., 4:162-64.

155. *Times and Seasons*, Vol. 2, 304-05.

156. Accounts of Phelps's return vary, but, for the purposes of telling this story, the author has chosen this touching scene.

157. Jenson, Andrew, *LDS Biographical Encyclopedia*, Vol. 3, 692.

158. Barrett, 504.

159. Van Wagoner, Richard and Walker, Steven C., "The Joseph/Hyrum Smith Funeral Sermon," *Brigham Young University Studies* 23 (Winter 1983).

160. Davidson, 55-56. The last two lines of the second stanza originally read: "Long may his blood, which was shed by assassins, / Stain Illinois while the earth lauds his fame." The 1985 version is of course different. See *Hymns*, no. 27.

161. *Hymns*, no. 27.

162. *Hymns*, no. 284; *A Book of Mormons*, 209.

BIBLIOGRAPHY

Arrington, Leonard J., "Joseph Smith, Builder of Ideal Communities," *The Prophet Joseph Smith—Essays on the Life and Mission of Joseph Smith,* Larry C. Porter and Susan Easton Black, eds. Salt Lake City: Deseret Book, 1988.

Backman, Milton V. and Cowan, Richard O. *Joseph Smith and the Doctrine and Covenants.* Salt Lake City: Deseret Book, 1992.

Barrett, Ivan J. *Joseph Smith and the Restoration: A History of the Church to 1846.* Provo: Brigham Young University Press, 1910.

Bowen, Walter Dean. *The Versatile W. W. Phelps: Mormon Writer, Educator, and Pioneer.* Master's thesis, Brigham Young University, 1958.

Brown, S. Kent, Cannon, Donald Q., and Jackson, Richard H., eds. *Historical Atlas of Mormonism.* New York City: Simon & Schuster, 1994.

Clark, James R., ed. *Messages of the First Presidency.* Salt Lake City: Bookcraft, 1965.

Cook, Lyndon W. *The Revelations of the Prophet Joseph Smith.* Salt Lake City: Deseret Book, 1985.

Davidson, Karen Lynn. *Our Latter-day Hymns, the Stories and the Messages.* Salt Lake City: Deseret Book, 1988.

Evans, John Henry. *One Hundred Years of Mormonism.* Salt Lake City: The Deseret News Press, 1905.

Hymns of The Church of Jesus Christ of Latter-day Saints. Salt Lake City: The Church of Jesus Christ of Latter-day Saints, 1985.

Jenson, Andrew. *LDS Biographical Encyclopedia.* Salt Lake City: Andrew Jenson History Co., 1920.

——. *Journal of Discourses.* 26 vols. London: Latter-day Saints' Book Depot, 1854–1886.

Ludlow, Daniel H., ed. *Encyclopedia of Mormonism.* 4 vols. New York: Macmillan Publishing Co., 1992.

McConkie, Bruce R. *A New Witness for the Articles of Faith.* Salt Lake City: Deseret Book, 1985.

——. *Mormon Doctrine.* Salt Lake City: Bookcraft, 1966.

Nibley, Hugh. "What Is Zion? A Distant View," *Approaching Zion.* Salt Lake City: Deseret Book & F.A.R.M.S., 1989.

Roberts, B. H. *Outlines of Ecclesiastical History.* Salt Lake City: The Church of Jesus Christ of Latter-day Saints, 1924.

——. *The Missouri Persecutions.* Salt Lake City: Bookcraft, 1965.

Salt Lake Temple Presidency. *The Salt Lake Temple: A Centennial Book of Remembrance, 1893–1993.* Salt Lake City: Privately published, 1993.

Smith, Joseph Fielding. *Answers to Gospel Questions,* 5 vols. Salt Lake City: Deseret Book, 1957.

——. *Church History and Modern Revelation.* Salt Lake City: The Church of Jesus Christ of Latter-day Saints, 1946.

——. *Doctrines of Salvation.* 3 vols. Salt Lake City: Bookcraft, 1954.

Smith, Joseph, *Teachings of the Prophet Joseph Smith,* sel. Joseph Fielding Smith. Salt Lake City: The Deseret News Press, 1938.

——. *History of the Church.* 7 vols. Salt Lake City: Deseret Book, 1951.

Van Wagoner, Richard S. and Walker, Steven C. *A Book of Mormons.* Salt Lake City: Signature Books, 1982.

LARRY BARKDULL has spent nearly twenty years publishing others' creative products. But in 1996 he published one of his own, the nationally acclaimed book *The Mourning Dove*. He comes now with his second book, *Praise to the Man*. A member of The Church of Jesus Christ of Latter-day Saints, Larry has served in many leadership positions. He and his wife, Elizabeth, reside in Orem, Utah, and are the parents of ten children.